準《 全新撰寫！
題目精準、刷題有感，考生一致推薦！

GEPT
全民英檢
中級複試 10回
高分模擬試題＋翻譯解答
寫作＆口說
【試題本】

　　全民英檢 2021 年 1 月改版新題型，內容主要針對初級、中級、中高級初試的聽力跟閱讀測驗做調整，而複試的寫作與口說測驗題型則不變。

　　有鑑於寫作與口說常是讀者最害怕的測驗類型，我們集結中外編輯群，經多次研擬並網羅各類新鮮題材或時事，終於完成這本**全新編寫、仿真度極高**的《**準！GEPT 全民英檢中級複試 10 回高分模擬試題 + 翻譯解答**》，希望藉由**反覆練習**以培養讀者的作答能力與經驗，真正上戰場時能夠從容不迫、輕鬆應戰。

　　寫作的部分，我們納入各種**日常情境**與**時事**，讓讀者從**生活經驗**出發，好寫好下筆。口說的部分，**題材新穎活潑、平易近人**並且聘請專業錄音員錄製音檔。我們也將音檔上傳雲端，只需掃描 QR Code 便能**隨時隨地聆聽**，音檔也採**多種分段的方式**，可依個人需求使用。

　　本書的內容除了提供讀者練習英檢寫作與口說之外，更期盼讀者能將有用的單詞、片語等記在腦海裡，尤其是近年的熱門單詞如 extrovert（外向的人）、introvert（內向的人）、artificial intelligence（AI）等等。此外，試題本前段所附上的作答攻略則是提供讀者準備的方向與策略。

　　祝各位學習成功！

Contents 目錄

中級全民英檢測驗複試簡介與作答攻略 ⋯ ii

Test 1
寫作能力測驗 ⋯⋯⋯⋯⋯⋯⋯⋯⋯⋯ 2
口說能力測驗　🔊 001 / 011-023 ⋯⋯ 4

Test 2
寫作能力測驗 ⋯⋯⋯⋯⋯⋯⋯⋯⋯⋯ 8
口說能力測驗　🔊 002 / 024-036 ⋯⋯ 10

Test 3
寫作能力測驗 ⋯⋯⋯⋯⋯⋯⋯⋯⋯⋯ 14
口說能力測驗　🔊 003 / 037-049 ⋯⋯ 16

Test 4
寫作能力測驗 ⋯⋯⋯⋯⋯⋯⋯⋯⋯⋯ 20
口說能力測驗　🔊 004 / 050-062 ⋯⋯ 22

Test 5
寫作能力測驗 ⋯⋯⋯⋯⋯⋯⋯⋯⋯⋯ 26
口說能力測驗　🔊 005 / 063-075 ⋯⋯ 28

Test 6
寫作能力測驗 ⋯⋯⋯⋯⋯⋯⋯⋯⋯⋯ 32
口說能力測驗　🔊 006 / 076-088 ⋯⋯ 34

Test 7
寫作能力測驗 ⋯⋯⋯⋯⋯⋯⋯⋯⋯⋯ 38
口說能力測驗　🔊 007 / 089-101 ⋯⋯ 40

Test 8
寫作能力測驗 ⋯⋯⋯⋯⋯⋯⋯⋯⋯⋯ 44
口說能力測驗　🔊 008 / 102-114 ⋯⋯ 46

Test 9
寫作能力測驗 ⋯⋯⋯⋯⋯⋯⋯⋯⋯⋯ 50
口說能力測驗　🔊 009 / 115-127 ⋯⋯ 52

Test 10
寫作能力測驗 ⋯⋯⋯⋯⋯⋯⋯⋯⋯⋯ 56
口說能力測驗　🔊 010 / 128-140 ⋯⋯ 58

附錄：測驗用答案紙 ⋯⋯⋯⋯⋯⋯⋯ 65

全書音檔 + 壓縮檔

中級全民英檢測驗複試簡介與作答攻略

◉ 簡介：英檢中級複試分為 2 個部分，分別為寫作能力測驗與口說能力測驗，資訊如下：

測驗項目	題型	題數	作答時間	通過標準／滿分
寫作能力測驗	第一部分 - 中譯英	1 段	40 分鐘	80分／100分
	第二部分 - 英文作文	1 篇		
口說能力測驗	第一部分 - 朗讀短文	2 段	15 分鐘	80分／100分
	第二部分 - 回答問題	10 題		
	第三部分 - 看圖敘述	1 張圖		

◉ 寫作能力測驗及口說能力測驗採人工閱卷，每份作答均由兩位評分人員進行初審與複審後，評定級分，成績為 0～5 級分，再轉換成百分制。

◉ 寫作能力測驗級分說明：

分數計算公式為

【(中譯英第一位評定級分＋中譯英第二位評定級分) ÷ 2 × 20 分 × 40%】＋【(英文作文第一位評定級分＋英文作文第二位評定級分) ÷ 2 × 20 分 × 60%】

範例

若某考生寫作部分得分為：中譯英第一位評為 4 級分、中譯英第二位評為 4 級分，英文作文第一位評為 4 級分、英文作文第二位評為 4 級分，經平均後轉換為百分制為 80 分
(【(4 級分 ＋ 4 級分) ÷ 2 × 20 分 × 40%】＋【(4 級分 ＋ 4 級分) ÷ 2 × 20 分 × 60%】＝ 32 分 ＋ 48 分 ＝ 80 分)。

寫作測驗作答攻略分享

中譯英

❶ 標點符號、大小寫、拼字正確、字跡工整為基本必備的條件。

❷ 注意**時態**：
先閱讀整個中文段落，確定作答的時態。並且注意句子間的時間順序，作出相對應的變化。

❸ 使用英文**句型**：
依據中文語意，判斷出可使用的英文句型，能使翻譯更為流暢、優美。

❹ **詞要達意**：
中英文之間的語意常有落差需注意，配合翻譯使用適當的**轉折詞**，使語句通順。

❺ Double Check：
寫完翻譯後務必將中英文再對過一次，確保萬無一失。

英文作文

❶ 對症下藥：
依據題目給的提示下筆，避免離題。

❷ 擬定**綱要**：
依據提示先擬定作文的綱要 —— 簡單列出，可用中文寫，若能用英文更好。文末應有適當結尾。

❸ 有靈感馬上寫下：
思考過程中若想到任何英文詞句，立刻寫在空白處，真正動筆時便能寫入。

❹ 其餘注意事項與中譯英的第 ❶ – ❺ 點相同。

 口說測驗作答攻略分享

朗讀短文

❶ 咬字要**清晰**，語速**適當**即可。

❷ 注意語氣的**抑揚頓挫**，避免機器人式的唸法。

❸ 注意與**數字**相關的唸法：若是西元年可唸為 2 個十位數較簡易也清楚 —— 如 2010 唸為 twenty-ten —— 此唸法沒有強制，依個人習慣為主；數字的單位也要注意 —— 如 NT$100 唸為 "one hundred NT dollars" 或 "one hundred New Taiwan dollars" 等等。

回答問題

❶ 第 1-5 題回答時間為 15 秒，約 **2-3 句話**結束；第 6-10 題回答時間為 30 秒，約 **4-6 句話**結束。建議讀者依自身語速實際測量調整。

❷ 回答時第一句話建議**直接回答問題**。如題目問 "Do you like hiking? Why or why not?"，回答時就先說 "Yes." 或 "No." 其後**務必再表述原因**，讓評分者更了解您的口語表達能力。

❸ 作答時間內盡量表達。

看圖敘述

❶ 作答前 30 秒的時間看圖及問題，在腦海中依題目順序模擬回答內容即可，**不能用筆寫下要回答的內容**（考試規定）。

❷ 發揮**隨機應變**的能力。遇到不會說的字，若可跳過就跳過，若一定得談到可盡量用自己知道的字代替，例如圖片中有「鴿子」，但湊巧不會說 dove / pigeon，那就說 bird，依此類推。

★ 練習口說時，建議讀者可將自己的回答用手機或錄音筆錄下，再回放聆聽，分析自己唸不好或回答不好的地方，思考過後再重來一次，如此反覆練習到完善的地步，然後用新的題目重新練習，如此一來必定能夠愈來愈進步。

GEPT 中級複試模擬測驗 第 ❶ 回
General English Proficiency Test — Intermediate Level Test 1

寫作能力測驗
第一部分：中譯英

第二部分：英文作文

口說能力測驗
第一部分：朗讀短文

第二部分：回答問題

第三部分：看圖敘述

TEST 1

寫作能力測驗

注意事項

① 本測驗共有兩部分。第一部分為中譯英,第二部分為英文作文。測驗時間為 **40 分鐘**。

② 請利用試題紙空白處及背面擬稿,但正答務必書寫在「寫作能力測驗答案紙」上。在答案紙以外的地方作答,不予計分。

③ 第一部分中譯英請在答案紙第一頁作答,第二部分英文作文請在答案紙第二頁作答。

④ 作答時請勿隔行書寫,請注意字跡應清晰可讀,並請保持答案紙之清潔,以免影響評分。

⑤ 測驗時,不得在准考證或其他物品上抄題,亦不得有傳遞、夾帶小抄、左顧右盼或交談等違規行為。

⑥ 意圖或已經將試卷攜出試場者,五年內不得報名參加本測驗。請人代考者,連同代考者,三年內不得報名參加本測驗。

⑦ 測驗結束時,須立即停止作答,在原位靜候監試人員收回全部試題紙及答案紙,清點無誤後,宣布結束始可離場。

⑧ 應試者入場、出場及測驗中如有違反上列規則或不服監試人員之指示者,監試人員得取消其應試資格並請其離場,且作答不予計分。

寫作能力測驗

本測驗共有兩部分。第一部分為中譯英，第二部分為英文作文。測驗時間為 **40 分鐘**。

第一部分：中譯英（40%）

說明：請將下列的一段中文翻譯成通順、達意且前後連貫的英文。

　　氣象預報說週末是好天氣，所以爸爸建議全家人利用這機會去山上露營。我們把帳篷塞進大包包裡，然後開車到老爸在網路上訂好的營地。那裡的景色非常壯觀。我們把帳篷搭起來，然後爸爸做了一頓簡單的晚飯，但卻非常好吃。晚上我們圍坐在營火旁觀賞晴朗夜空中的流星。這真是一次令人難忘的露營之旅。

第二部分：英文作文（60%）

說明：請依下面所提供的文字提示寫一篇英文作文，長度約 120 字（8 至 12 個句子）。作文可以是一個完整的段落，也可以分段。（評分重點包括內容、組織、文法、用字遣詞、標點符號、大小寫。）

提示：當我們在發育時，最需要的就是吃得健康、吃得營養。尤其是在求學階段，我們更需要關注學校所提供的餐點。請寫一篇文章
❶ 請問你在學校吃的是健康的餐點嗎？
❷ 學校該如何鼓勵學生吃得健康？

TEST 1

本回完整音檔 🔊 001
本回分段音檔 🔊 011~023

口說能力測驗

注意事項

① 本測驗問題由耳機播放,回答則經麥克風錄下。分朗讀短文、回答問題與看圖敘述三部分,時間共約 15 分鐘,連同口試說明時間共需約五十分鐘。

② 第一部分朗讀短文有 1 分鐘準備時間,此時請勿唸出聲音,待聽到"請開始朗讀" 2 分鐘的朗讀時間開始時,再將短文唸出來。第二部分回答問題的題目將播出二遍,聽完第二次題目後要立即回答。第三部分看圖敘述有 30 秒的思考時間及 1 分 30 秒的答題時間,思考時不可在試題紙上作記號,亦不可發出聲音。等聽到指示開始回答時,請您針對圖片在作答時間內盡量的回答。

③ 錄音設備皆已事先完成設定,請勿觸動任何機件,以免影響錄音。測驗時請戴妥耳機,將麥克風調到嘴邊約三公分處,聽清楚說明,依指示以適中音量回答。

④ 評分人員將根據您錄下的回答(發音與語調、語法與字彙、可解度及切題度等)作整體的評分。您可利用所附音檔自行測試,一一錄下回答後,再播出來聽聽,並斟酌調整。練習時請儘量以英語思考、應對,考試時較易有自然的表現。

⑤ 請注意測驗時不可在試題紙上劃線、打"✓"或作任何記號;不可在准考證或其他物品上抄題;亦不可有傳遞、夾帶小抄、左顧右盼或交談等違規行為。

⑥ 意圖或已將試題紙或試題影音資料攜出或傳送出試場者,視同侵犯本中心著作財產權,限五年內不得報名參加「全民英檢」測驗。請人代考者,連同代考者,三年內不得報名參加本測驗。

⑦ 測驗結束時,須立即停止作答,在原位靜候監試人員收回全部試題紙且清點無誤,等候監試人員宣布結束後始可離場。

⑧ 入場、出場及測驗中如有違反上列規則或不服監試人員之指示者,監試人員將取消您的應試資格並請您離場,且作答不予計分,亦不退費。

口說能力測驗

請在 **15** 秒內完成並唸出下列自我介紹的句子：
My seat number is（座位號碼後 5 碼）, and my registration number is（准考證號碼後 5 碼）.

TEST
1

第一部分：朗讀短文　🔊 011

請先利用一分鐘的時間閱讀下面的短文，然後在二分鐘內以正常的速度，清楚正確的讀出下面的短文，閱讀時請不要發出聲音。

　　I usually get a ride to school, so I rarely need to take the bus. This morning, though, my regular ride wasn't available. Therefore, I had to take public transportation during rush hour. It felt like there were thousands of people on my bus, and we were all crammed together. The traffic was awful, too, so the journey seemed to take forever. To make matters worse, it was raining, so everyone was carrying wet umbrellas. I hope my ride is available tomorrow!

＊　　　　　　＊　　　　　　＊

　　As many countries try to reduce their dependence on fossil fuels, they are using more and more renewable energy sources. Two common sources are solar and wind power. Solar energy involves using the sunlight to create electricity through solar panels. This type of energy is clean, but it relies heavily on sunny weather. Wind energy, on the other hand, uses wind turbines to change the power of the wind into electricity. It, too, is dependent on the weather, and some people find wind turbines noisy and ugly.

第二部分：回答問題　🔊 012-022

共十題。題目已事先錄音，每題經由耳機播出二次，不印在試卷上。第一至五題，每題回答時間 15 秒；第六至十題，每題回答時間 30 秒。每題播出後，請立即回答。回答時，不一定要用完整的句子，但請在作答時間內盡量的表達。

TEST 1

第三部分：看圖敘述　🔊 023

下面有一張圖片及四個相關的問題，請在一分半鐘內完成作答。作答時，請直接回答，不需將題號及題目唸出。

首先請利用 30 秒的時間看圖及問題。

❶ 這可能是什麼地方？
❷ 圖片中的這些人在做什麼？
❸ 你曾經利用過這樣的服務嗎？為什麼？
❹ 如果還有時間，請詳細描述圖片中的景物。

請將下列自我介紹的句子再唸一遍：

My seat number is (座位號碼後 5 碼), and my registration number is (准考證號碼後 5 碼).

GEPT 中級複試模擬測驗　第 ❷ 回
General English Proficiency Test — Intermediate Level Test 2

寫作能力測驗
第一部分：中譯英
第二部分：英文作文

口說能力測驗
第一部分：朗讀短文
第二部分：回答問題
第三部分：看圖敘述

TEST 2

寫作能力測驗

注意事項

① 本測驗共有兩部分。第一部分為中譯英，第二部分為英文作文。測驗時間為 **40 分鐘**。

② 請利用試題紙空白處及背面擬稿，但正答務必書寫在「寫作能力測驗答案紙」上。在答案紙以外的地方作答，不予計分。

③ 第一部分中譯英請在答案紙第一頁作答，第二部分英文作文請在答案紙第二頁作答。

④ 作答時請勿隔行書寫，請注意字跡應清晰可讀，並請保持答案紙之清潔，以免影響評分。

⑤ 測驗時，不得在准考證或其他物品上抄題，亦不得有傳遞、夾帶小抄、左顧右盼或交談等違規行為。

⑥ 意圖或已經將試卷攜出試場者，五年內不得報名參加本測驗。請人代考者，連同代考者，三年內不得報名參加本測驗。

⑦ 測驗結束時，須立即停止作答，在原位靜候監試人員收回全部試題紙及答案紙，清點無誤後，宣布結束始可離場。

⑧ 應試者入場、出場及測驗中如有違反上列規則或不服監試人員之指示者，監試人員得取消其應試資格並請其離場，且作答不予計分。

寫作能力測驗

本測驗共有兩部分。第一部分為中譯英，第二部分為英文作文。測驗時間為 **40 分鐘**。

第一部分：中譯英（40%）

說明：請將下列的一段中文翻譯成通順、達意且前後連貫的英文。

　　朗達（Rhonda）在最新款的 iPhone 發售當天就跑去排隊買。她買到了當天那家分店的最後一支 iPhone 超興奮，迫不及待想回家開始連上 Wi-Fi 玩一整天的遊戲。很不巧她錯過了一班公車，而且下一班一小時後才會來！當她終於到家時，她的同事 call 她一起去打籃球。朗達勉為其難地答應去打球，但她真正想做的是玩她的新手機啊！

第二部分：英文作文（60%）

說明：請依下面所提供的文字提示寫一篇英文作文，長度約 120 字（8 至 12 個句子）。作文可以是一個完整的段落，也可以分段。（評分重點包括內容、組織、文法、用字遣詞、標點符號、大小寫。）

提示：有些人在閒暇的時候特別喜歡主動去認識不同的朋友，有些人則只喜歡與自己相處。請寫一篇文章

❶ 你是外向的人還是內向的人？
❷ 你喜歡與人社交嗎？為什麼？

TEST 2

本回完整音檔 🔊 002
本回分段音檔 🔊 024~036

口說能力測驗

注意事項

① 本測驗問題由耳機播放，回答則經麥克風錄下。分朗讀短文、回答問題與看圖敘述三部分，時間共約 15 分鐘，連同口試說明時間共需約五十分鐘。

② 第一部分朗讀短文有 1 分鐘準備時間，此時請勿唸出聲音，待聽到"請開始朗讀" 2 分鐘的朗讀時間開始時，再將短文唸出來。第二部分回答問題的題目將播出二遍，聽完第二次題目後要立即回答。第三部分看圖敘述有 30 秒的思考時間及 1 分 30 秒的答題時間，思考時不可在試題紙上作記號，亦不可發出聲音。等聽到指示開始回答時，請您針對圖片在作答時間內盡量的回答。

③ 錄音設備皆已事先完成設定，請勿觸動任何機件，以免影響錄音。測驗時請戴妥耳機，將麥克風調到嘴邊約三公分處，聽清楚說明，依指示以適中音量回答。

④ 評分人員將根據您錄下的回答（發音與語調、語法與字彙、可解度及切題度等）作整體的評分。您可利用所附音檔自行測試，一一錄下回答後，再播出來聽聽，並斟酌調整。練習時請儘量以英語思考、應對，考試時較易有自然的表現。

⑤ 請注意測驗時不可在試題紙上劃線、打"✓"或作任何記號；不可在准考證或其他物品上抄題；亦不可有傳遞、夾帶小抄、左顧右盼或交談等違規行為。

⑥ 意圖或已將試題紙或試題影音資料攜出或傳送出試場者，視同侵犯本中心著作財產權，限五年內不得報名參加「全民英檢」測驗。請人代考者，連同代考者，三年內不得報名參加本測驗。

⑦ 測驗結束時，須立即停止作答，在原位靜候監試人員收回全部試題紙且清點無誤，等候監試人員宣布結束後始可離場。

⑧ 入場、出場及測驗中如有違反上列規則或不服監試人員之指示者，監試人員將取消您的應試資格並請您離場，且作答不予計分，亦不退費。

請在 **15** 秒內完成並唸出下列自我介紹的句子：
My seat number is（座位號碼後 5 碼）, and my registration number is（准考證號碼後 5 碼）.

第一部分：朗讀短文 🔊 024

請先利用一分鐘的時間閱讀下面的短文，然後在二分鐘內以正常的速度，清楚正確的讀出下面的短文，閱讀時請不要發出聲音。

Rita is organizing a surprise birthday party for her best friend Jenny. She has found a suitable location and bought some balloons which will be used to decorate the place. She has pre-ordered the food from a local restaurant that Jenny frequently goes to. She has also hired a DJ and informed him of Jenny's favorite tunes. Now all she needs to do is send out invitations to their classmates and pray that no one spills the beans about the celebration.

　　　　＊　　　　　　＊　　　　　　＊

The first cell phone was invented around five decades ago, but it was not until the 1990s that these devices became small and portable enough to be used extensively. At this time, people could send text messages, play elementary games, and use functions like calendars and reminders on their phones. It was not until 2007 that the smartphone, as many people would call it, came into being. Combining a touchscreen with internet access and downloadable apps, the smartphone transformed the communications and electronics industries.

第二部分：回答問題 🔊 025-035

共十題。題目已事先錄音，每題經由耳機播出二次，不印在試卷上。第一至五題，每題回答時間 15 秒；第六至十題，每題回答時間 30 秒。每題播出後，請立即回答。回答時，不一定要用完整的句子，但請在作答時間內盡量的表達。

第三部分：看圖敘述　📢 036

下面有一張圖片及四個相關的問題，請在一分半鐘內完成作答。作答時，請直接回答，不需將題號及題目唸出。

首先請利用 30 秒的時間看圖及問題。

❶ 這可能是什麼地方？
❷ 圖片中的這些人在做什麼？
❸ 你喜歡去這種場所嗎？你會有怎樣的感受？
❹ 如果還有時間，請詳細描述圖片中的景物。

請將下列自我介紹的句子再唸一遍：
My seat number is（座位號碼後 5 碼）, and my registration number is（准考證號碼後 5 碼）.

GEPT 中級複試模擬測驗　第 ❸ 回
General English Proficiency Test — Intermediate Level Test 3

寫作能力測驗

第一部分：中譯英

第二部分：英文作文

口說能力測驗

第一部分：朗讀短文

第二部分：回答問題

第三部分：看圖敘述

TEST 3

寫作能力測驗

注意事項

① 本測驗共有兩部分。第一部分為中譯英，第二部分為英文作文。測驗時間為 **40 分鐘**。

② 請利用試題紙空白處及背面擬稿，但正答務必書寫在「寫作能力測驗答案紙」上。在答案紙以外的地方作答，不予計分。

③ 第一部分中譯英請在答案紙第一頁作答，第二部分英文作文請在答案紙第二頁作答。

④ 作答時請勿隔行書寫，請注意字跡應清晰可讀，並請保持答案紙之清潔，以免影響評分。

⑤ 測驗時，不得在准考證或其他物品上抄題，亦不得有傳遞、夾帶小抄、左顧右盼或交談等違規行為。

⑥ 意圖或已經將試卷攜出試場者，五年內不得報名參加本測驗。請人代考者，連同代考者，三年內不得報名參加本測驗。

⑦ 測驗結束時，須立即停止作答，在原位靜候監試人員收回全部試題紙及答案紙，清點無誤後，宣布結束始可離場。

⑧ 應試者入場、出場及測驗中如有違反上列規則或不服監試人員之指示者，監試人員得取消其應試資格並請其離場，且作答不予計分。

本測驗共有兩部分。第一部分為中譯英，第二部分為英文作文。測驗時間為 **40 分鐘**。

第一部分：中譯英（40%）

說明：請將下列的一段中文翻譯成通順、達意且前後連貫的英文。

　　彼得（Peter）退休時很擔心人生會失去目標。因此他決定要參與慈善志工服務。雖然捐錢又快又簡單，但他想要奉獻他的時間。他選擇了一間幫助窮苦三餐不繼民眾的地方慈善機構。他首先主辦了一場烘焙義賣來募款。後來他協助將超市捐贈的食物打包裝盒。彼得感到很滿足，因為他可以在社區裡幫助那些需要幫助的人。

第二部分：英文作文（60%）

說明：請依下面所提供的文字提示寫一篇英文作文，長度約 120 字（8 至 12 個句子）。作文可以是一個完整的段落，也可以分段。（評分重點包括內容、組織、文法、用字遣詞、標點符號、大小寫。）

提示：每到旅遊旺季的期間，各地都充滿著觀光客，大家都想趁機放鬆一下，並且為自己留下美好的回憶。請寫一篇文章
❶ 你旅行時喜歡買紀念品嗎？為什麼？
❷ 如果有，哪一個紀念品對你來說最特別？如果沒有，你會以什麼方式回憶每次的旅行？

TEST 3

本回完整音檔 🔊 003
本回分段音檔 🔊 037~049

口說能力測驗

注意事項

① 本測驗問題由耳機播放，回答則經麥克風錄下。分朗讀短文、回答問題與看圖敘述三部分，時間共約 15 分鐘，連同口試說明時間共需約五十分鐘。

② 第一部分朗讀短文有 1 分鐘準備時間，此時請勿唸出聲音，待聽到 "請開始朗讀" 2 分鐘的朗讀時間開始時，再將短文唸出來。第二部分回答問題的題目將播出二遍，聽完第二次題目後要立即回答。第三部分看圖敘述有 30 秒的思考時間及 1 分 30 秒的答題時間，思考時不可在試題紙上作記號，亦不可發出聲音。等聽到指示開始回答時，請您針對圖片在作答時間內盡量的回答。

③ 錄音設備皆已事先完成設定，請勿觸動任何機件，以免影響錄音。測驗時請戴妥耳機，將麥克風調到嘴邊約三公分處，聽清楚說明，依指示以適中音量回答。

④ 評分人員將根據您錄下的回答（發音與語調、語法與字彙、可解度及切題度等）作整體的評分。您可利用所附音檔自行測試，一一錄下回答後，再播出來聽聽，並斟酌調整。練習時請儘量以英語思考、應對，考試時較易有自然的表現。

⑤ 請注意測驗時不可在試題紙上劃線、打 "✓" 或作任何記號；不可在准考證或其他物品上抄題；亦不可有傳遞、夾帶小抄、左顧右盼或交談等違規行為。

⑥ 意圖或已將試題紙或試題影音資料攜出或傳送出試場者，視同侵犯本中心著作財產權，限五年內不得報名參加「全民英檢」測驗。請人代考者，連同代考者，三年內不得報名參加本測驗。

⑦ 測驗結束時，須立即停止作答，在原位靜候監試人員收回全部試題紙且清點無誤，等候監試人員宣布結束後始可離場。

⑧ 入場、出場及測驗中如有違反上列規則或不服監試人員之指示者，監試人員將取消您的應試資格並請您離場，且作答不予計分，亦不退費。

請在 **15** 秒內完成並唸出下列自我介紹的句子：
My seat number is（座位號碼後 5 碼）, and my registration number is（准考證號碼後 5 碼）.

第一部分：朗讀短文 🔊 037

請先利用一分鐘的時間閱讀下面的短文，然後在二分鐘內以正常的速度，清楚正確的讀出下面的短文，閱讀時請不要發出聲音。

Earlier this year, I went to Germany with my older brother. He intends to study there someday and wanted to learn more about the place. He really enjoyed traveling around the country, and I did too. However, after a few days, I began to miss Taiwanese food, especially my mom's cooking. I got tired of the freezing weather and being unable to speak the language. I realized that I had a serious case of homesickness. I couldn't wait to go back to Taiwan—a warm place with the best food in the world.

* * *

Museums play an essential role in preserving history. They collect objects from the past and ensure these are kept safe for future generations. They store everything from historical documents to paintings to ancient tools, all of which give visitors a glimpse into different cultures, societies, and time periods. Museums serve as a vital educational resource, helping to make sure that we learn the lessons of the past and reducing our chances of repeating our ancestors' mistakes.

第二部分：回答問題 🔊 038-048

共十題。題目已事先錄音，每題經由耳機播出二次，不印在試卷上。第一至五題，每題回答時間 15 秒；第六至十題，每題回答時間 30 秒。每題播出後，請立即回答。回答時，不一定要用完整的句子，但請在作答時間內盡量的表達。

TEST 3

第三部分：看圖敘述 🔊 049

下面有一張圖片及四個相關的問題，請在一分半鐘內完成作答。作答時，請直接回答，不需將題號及題目唸出。

首先請利用 30 秒的時間看圖及問題。

❶ 圖片中的這些人在做什麼？
❷ 這可能是什麼地方？
❸ 你時常從事這樣的活動嗎？為什麼？
❹ 如果還有時間，請詳細描述圖片中的景物。

請將下列自我介紹的句子再唸一遍：

My seat number is (座位號碼後 5 碼), and my registration number is (准考證號碼後 5 碼).

GEPT 中級複試模擬測驗 第 ❹ 回
General English Proficiency Test — Intermediate Level Test 4

寫作能力測驗
第一部分：中譯英

第二部分：英文作文

口說能力測驗
第一部分：朗讀短文

第二部分：回答問題

第三部分：看圖敘述

TEST 4

寫作能力測驗

注意事項

① 本測驗共有兩部分。第一部分為中譯英,第二部分為英文作文。測驗時間為 **40 分鐘**。

② 請利用試題紙空白處及背面擬稿,但正答務必書寫在「寫作能力測驗答案紙」上。在答案紙以外的地方作答,不予計分。

③ 第一部分中譯英請在答案紙第一頁作答,第二部分英文作文請在答案紙第二頁作答。

④ 作答時請勿隔行書寫,請注意字跡應清晰可讀,並請保持答案紙之清潔,以免影響評分。

⑤ 測驗時,不得在准考證或其他物品上抄題,亦不得有傳遞、夾帶小抄、左顧右盼或交談等違規行為。

⑥ 意圖或已經將試卷攜出試場者,五年內不得報名參加本測驗。請人代考者,連同代考者,三年內不得報名參加本測驗。

⑦ 測驗結束時,須立即停止作答,在原位靜候監試人員收回全部試題紙及答案紙,清點無誤後,宣布結束始可離場。

⑧ 應試者入場、出場及測驗中如有違反上列規則或不服監試人員之指示者,監試人員得取消其應試資格並請其離場,且作答不予計分。

第一部分：中譯英（40%）

說明：請將下列的一段中文翻譯成通順、達意且前後連貫的英文。

我週末時去了一個農民市集，是個在地農民把農產品直接銷售給大眾的地方。那裡有非常多攤販兜售各式各樣的食物，看起來都很好吃的樣子，香味撲鼻而來。我試吃了幾樣我最喜歡的東西：有起司、有香腸，也喝了在地生產的葡萄酒。我買了些新鮮蔬果，這個禮拜就不愁沒有營養的食材可煮了！如果你家附近有農民市集的話，我強烈建議去那裡逛逛。

第二部分：英文作文（60%）

說明：請依下面所提供的文字提示寫一篇英文作文，長度約 120 字（8 至 12 個句子）。作文可以是一個完整的段落，也可以分段。（評分重點包括內容、組織、文法、用字遣詞、標點符號、大小寫。）

提示：最近這幾年，許多企業紛紛投入發展人工智慧，也有許多人開始將人工智慧應用在生活中。
請寫一篇文章
❶ 就你所知，使用人工智慧的好處與壞處分別是什麼？
❷ 你有在使用人工智慧協助你嗎？為什麼？

TEST 4

 本回完整音檔 ◀))004
本回分段音檔 ◀))050~062

口說能力測驗

注意事項

① 本測驗問題由耳機播放，回答則經麥克風錄下。分朗讀短文、回答問題與看圖敘述三部分，時間共約 15 分鐘，連同口試說明時間共需約五十分鐘。

② 第一部分朗讀短文有 1 分鐘準備時間，此時請勿唸出聲音，待聽到"請開始朗讀" 2 分鐘的朗讀時間開始時，再將短文唸出來。第二部分回答問題的題目將播出二遍，聽完第二次題目後要立即回答。第三部分看圖敘述有 30 秒的思考時間及 1 分 30 秒的答題時間，思考時不可在試題紙上作記號，亦不可發出聲音。等聽到指示開始回答時，請您針對圖片在作答時間內盡量的回答。

③ 錄音設備皆已事先完成設定，請勿觸動任何機件，以免影響錄音。測驗時請戴妥耳機，將麥克風調到嘴邊約三公分處，聽清楚說明，依指示以適中音量回答。

④ 評分人員將根據您錄下的回答（發音與語調、語法與字彙、可解度及切題度等）作整體的評分。您可利用所附音檔自行測試，一一錄下回答後，再播出來聽聽，並斟酌調整。練習時請儘量以英語思考、應對，考試時較易有自然的表現。

⑤ 請注意測驗時不可在試題紙上劃線、打"✓"或作任何記號；不可在准考證或其他物品上抄題；亦不可有傳遞、夾帶小抄、左顧右盼或交談等違規行為。

⑥ 意圖或已將試題紙或試題影音資料攜出或傳送出試場者，視同侵犯本中心著作財產權，限五年內不得報名參加「全民英檢」測驗。請人代考者，連同代考者，三年內不得報名參加本測驗。

⑦ 測驗結束時，須立即停止作答，在原位靜候監試人員收回全部試題紙且清點無誤，等候監試人員宣布結束後始可離場。

⑧ 入場、出場及測驗中如有違反上列規則或不服監試人員之指示者，監試人員將取消您的應試資格並請您離場，且作答不予計分，亦不退費。

請在 15 秒內完成並唸出下列自我介紹的句子：
My seat number is（座位號碼後 5 碼）, and my registration number is（准考證號碼後 5 碼）.

第一部分：朗讀短文 🔊 050

請先利用一分鐘的時間閱讀下面的短文，然後在二分鐘內以正常的速度，清楚正確的讀出下面的短文，閱讀時請不要發出聲音。

Paul never really wanted to learn how to swim. He felt somewhat scared of the water and much preferred to stay on dry land. Nevertheless, his parents, believing swimming to be an essential skill, forced him to take lessons. While being monitored by a swimming instructor, Paul reluctantly got in the swimming pool for the first time. To his surprise, he loved every second of the experience. Even more amazingly, he discovered that he had a natural talent for swimming.

* * *

Climate change is having a major impact on wildlife around the world. Some species are dealing with the loss of their natural environments. Polar bears, for instance, are reacting to melting ice by traveling longer distances to seek sources of food. Other species are experiencing changes in their natural cycles. Birds, for example, are arriving in their winter destinations too late for sufficient food to be available. This causes a chain reaction on other creatures in the food chain that depend on them.

第二部分：回答問題 🔊 051-061

共十題。題目已事先錄音，每題經由耳機播出二次，不印在試卷上。第一至五題，每題回答時間 15 秒；第六至十題，每題回答時間 30 秒。每題播出後，請立即回答。回答時，不一定要用完整的句子，但請在作答時間內盡量的表達。

TEST 4

第三部分：看圖敘述 🔊 062

下面有一張圖片及四個相關的問題，請在一分半鐘內完成作答。作答時，請直接回答，不需將題號及題目唸出。

首先請利用 30 秒的時間看圖及問題。

❶ 這可能是什麼地方？
❷ 圖片中的這些人在做什麼？
❸ 你覺得這麼做安全嗎？為什麼？
❹ 如果還有時間，請詳細描述圖片中的景物。

請將下列自我介紹的句子再唸一遍：

My seat number is (座位號碼後 5 碼), and my registration number is (准考證號碼後 5 碼).

GEPT 中級複試模擬測驗 第 ❺ 回
General English Proficiency Test — Intermediate Level Test 5

寫作能力測驗
- 第一部分：中譯英
- 第二部分：英文作文

口說能力測驗
- 第一部分：朗讀短文
- 第二部分：回答問題
- 第三部分：看圖敘述

TEST 5

寫作能力測驗

注意事項

① 本測驗共有兩部分。第一部分為中譯英，第二部分為英文作文。測驗時間為 **40 分鐘**。

② 請利用試題紙空白處及背面擬稿，但正答務必書寫在「寫作能力測驗答案紙」上。在答案紙以外的地方作答，不予計分。

③ 第一部分中譯英請在答案紙第一頁作答，第二部分英文作文請在答案紙第二頁作答。

④ 作答時請勿隔行書寫，請注意字跡應清晰可讀，並請保持答案紙之清潔，以免影響評分。

⑤ 測驗時，不得在准考證或其他物品上抄題，亦不得有傳遞、夾帶小抄、左顧右盼或交談等違規行為。

⑥ 意圖或已經將試卷攜出試場者，五年內不得報名參加本測驗。請人代考者，連同代考者，三年內不得報名參加本測驗。

⑦ 測驗結束時，須立即停止作答，在原位靜候監試人員收回全部試題紙及答案紙，清點無誤後，宣布結束始可離場。

⑧ 應試者入場、出場及測驗中如有違反上列規則或不服監試人員之指示者，監試人員得取消其應試資格並請其離場，且作答不予計分。

寫作能力測驗

本測驗共有兩部分。第一部分為中譯英，第二部分為英文作文。測驗時間為 **40 分鐘**。

第一部分：中譯英（40%）

說明：請將下列的一段中文翻譯成通順、達意且前後連貫的英文。

　　艾蜜莉亞（Amelia）的鄰居臨時要去出差，於是拜託她在此期間幫忙顧一下他的狗狗。艾蜜莉亞想到要照顧另一個生命，感到有點惶恐，但她覺得該幫鄰居的忙，所以就答應承擔這個責任。接下來七天，她遛狗、餵狗，還跟狗狗玩。原本艾蜜莉亞並未期待會跟那隻狗產生感情。然而他們倆很快就成了最好的朋友。當艾蜜莉亞的鄰居回來後，她立刻就去領養了一隻小狗！

TEST 5

第二部分：英文作文（60%）

說明：請依下面所提供的文字提示寫一篇英文作文，長度約 120 字（8 至 12 個句子）。作文可以是一個完整的段落，也可以分段。（評分重點包括內容、組織、文法、用字遣詞、標點符號、大小寫。）

提示：在博物館與美術館等地，一年四季都會有各類的展覽供民眾參觀，多多參觀展覽是個增廣見聞的好方法。請寫一篇文章
❶ 你喜歡參觀各類展覽嗎？為什麼？
❷ 你上一次參觀展覽是什麼時候？展覽的主題是什麼？

TEST 5

本回完整音檔 🔊 005
本回分段音檔 🔊 063~075

口說能力測驗

注意事項

① 本測驗問題由耳機播放，回答則經麥克風錄下。分朗讀短文、回答問題與看圖敘述三部分，時間共約 15 分鐘，連同口試說明時間共需約五十分鐘。

② 第一部分朗讀短文有 1 分鐘準備時間，此時請勿唸出聲音，待聽到"請開始朗讀" 2 分鐘的朗讀時間開始時，再將短文唸出來。第二部分回答問題的題目將播出二遍，聽完第二次題目後要立即回答。第三部分看圖敘述有 30 秒的思考時間及 1 分 30 秒的答題時間，思考時不可在試題紙上作記號，亦不可發出聲音。等聽到指示開始回答時，請您針對圖片在作答時間內盡量的回答。

③ 錄音設備皆已事先完成設定，請勿觸動任何機件，以免影響錄音。測驗時請戴妥耳機，將麥克風調到嘴邊約三公分處，聽清楚說明，依指示以適中音量回答。

④ 評分人員將根據您錄下的回答（發音與語調、語法與字彙、可解度及切題度等）作整體的評分。您可利用所附音檔自行測試，一一錄下回答後，再播出來聽聽，並斟酌調整。練習時請儘量以英語思考、應對，考試時較易有自然的表現。

⑤ 請注意測驗時不可在試題紙上劃線、打"✓"或作任何記號；不可在准考證或其他物品上抄題；亦不可有傳遞、夾帶小抄、左顧右盼或交談等違規行為。

⑥ 意圖或已將試題紙或試題影音資料攜出或傳送出試場者，視同侵犯本中心著作財產權，限五年內不得報名參加「全民英檢」測驗。請人代考者，連同代考者，三年內不得報名參加本測驗。

⑦ 測驗結束時，須立即停止作答，在原位靜候監試人員收回全部試題紙且清點無誤，等候監試人員宣布結束後始可離場。

⑧ 入場、出場及測驗中如有違反上列規則或不服監試人員之指示者，監試人員將取消您的應試資格並請您離場，且作答不予計分，亦不退費。

口說能力測驗

請在 15 秒內完成並唸出下列自我介紹的句子：
My seat number is （座位號碼後 5 碼）, and my registration number is （准考證號碼後 5 碼）.

第一部分：朗讀短文 🔊 063

請先利用一分鐘的時間閱讀下面的短文，然後在二分鐘內以正常的速度，清楚正確的讀出下面的短文，閱讀時請不要發出聲音。

My dad used to be an Uber driver. However, he found that sitting down and driving all day was giving him health problems, particularly with his back. He therefore quit the job and concentrated for a time on exercising and strengthening his back. Many people remarked that he looked significantly younger and fitter. So, he decided to become a fitness coach and help others achieve their fitness goals through a wide range of training programs. He loves his new career!

*　　　　　　*　　　　　　*

Florida and Taiwan are not typically mentioned in the same breath. The former covers around 170,000 square kilometers, is mainly flat, and has a consistently warm climate throughout the year. The latter covers 36,000 square kilometers, has many mountainous regions, and has a more varied climate with distinct seasons. Nevertheless, it is possible to identify some similarities between the two. For example, they both get hit by tropical storms, and they are both ideal destinations for seafood lovers and water sports fans.

第二部分：回答問題 🔊 064-074

共十題。題目已事先錄音，每題經由耳機播出二次，不印在試卷上。第一至五題，每題回答時間 15 秒；第六至十題，每題回答時間 30 秒。每題播出後，請立即回答。回答時，不一定要用完整的句子，但請在作答時間內盡量的表達。

TEST 5

第三部分：看圖敘述 🔊 075

下面有一張圖片及四個相關的問題，請在一分半鐘內完成作答。作答時，請直接回答，不需將題號及題目唸出。

首先請利用 30 秒的時間看圖及問題。

❶ 這可能是什麼地方？
❷ 圖片中的這些人在做什麼？
❸ 你曾經嘗試過這樣的活動嗎？為什麼？
❹ 如果還有時間，請詳細描述圖片中的景物。

請將下列自我介紹的句子再唸一遍：

My seat number is（座位號碼後 5 碼）, and my registration number is（准考證號碼後 5 碼）.

GEPT 中級複試模擬測驗 第 ❻ 回
General English Proficiency Test — Intermediate Level Test 6

寫作能力測驗
第一部分：中譯英

第二部分：英文作文

口說能力測驗
第一部分：朗讀短文

第二部分：回答問題

第三部分：看圖敘述

寫作能力測驗

注意事項

① 本測驗共有兩部分。第一部分為中譯英,第二部分為英文作文。測驗時間為 **40 分鐘**。

② 請利用試題紙空白處及背面擬稿,但正答務必書寫在「寫作能力測驗答案紙」上。在答案紙以外的地方作答,不予計分。

③ 第一部分中譯英請在答案紙第一頁作答,第二部分英文作文請在答案紙第二頁作答。

④ 作答時請勿隔行書寫,請注意字跡應清晰可讀,並請保持答案紙之清潔,以免影響評分。

⑤ 測驗時,不得在准考證或其他物品上抄題,亦不得有傳遞、夾帶小抄、左顧右盼或交談等違規行為。

⑥ 意圖或已經將試卷攜出試場者,五年內不得報名參加本測驗。請人代考者,連同代考者,三年內不得報名參加本測驗。

⑦ 測驗結束時,須立即停止作答,在原位靜候監試人員收回全部試題紙及答案紙,清點無誤後,宣布結束始可離場。

⑧ 應試者入場、出場及測驗中如有違反上列規則或不服監試人員之指示者,監試人員得取消其應試資格並請其離場,且作答不予計分。

寫作能力測驗

本測驗共有兩部分。第一部分為中譯英，第二部分為英文作文。測驗時間為 **40 分鐘**。

第一部分：中譯英（40%）

說明：請將下列的一段中文翻譯成通順、達意且前後連貫的英文。

傑洛米（Jeremy）第一次去巴黎的時候，以為可以光靠手機就能在市區各地趴趴走。他打算利用咖啡館和餐廳裡的免費 Wi-Fi 來規劃他從景點 A 到景點 B 的路線。然而他沒注意到他的手機沒電了，而他正在一處鳥不生蛋的郊區！於是他不得不轉換到替代方案：他得要去買一本地圖！

第二部分：英文作文（60%）

說明：請依下面所提供的文字提示寫一篇英文作文，長度約 120 字（8 至 12 個句子）。作文可以是一個完整的段落，也可以分段。（評分重點包括內容、組織、文法、用字遣詞、標點符號、大小寫。）

提示：各地的城市有各自不同的特色與魅力，有些城市生活很方便，有些則非常有文藝氣息。請寫一篇文章
❶ 一個適合居住的城市需要有哪些條件？
❷ 你未來想要搬到哪裡住？

TEST
6

TEST 6

口說能力測驗

本回完整音檔 📢 006
本回分段音檔 📢 076~088

注意事項

① 本測驗問題由耳機播放，回答則經麥克風錄下。分朗讀短文、回答問題與看圖敘述三部分，時間共約 15 分鐘，連同口試說明時間共需約五十分鐘。

② 第一部分朗讀短文有 1 分鐘準備時間，此時請勿唸出聲音，待聽到"請開始朗讀" 2 分鐘的朗讀時間開始時，再將短文唸出來。第二部分回答問題的題目將播出二遍，聽完第二次題目後要立即回答。第三部分看圖敘述有 30 秒的思考時間及 1 分 30 秒的答題時間，思考時不可在試題紙上作記號，亦不可發出聲音。等聽到指示開始回答時，請您針對圖片在作答時間內盡量的回答。

③ 錄音設備皆已事先完成設定，請勿觸動任何機件，以免影響錄音。測驗時請戴妥耳機，將麥克風調到嘴邊約三公分處，聽清楚說明，依指示以適中音量回答。

④ 評分人員將根據您錄下的回答（發音與語調、語法與字彙、可解度及切題度等）作整體的評分。您可利用所附音檔自行測試，一一錄下回答後，再播出來聽聽，並斟酌調整。練習時請儘量以英語思考、應對，考試時較易有自然的表現。

⑤ 請注意測驗時不可在試題紙上劃線、打"✓"或作任何記號；不可在准考證或其他物品上抄題；亦不可有傳遞、夾帶小抄、左顧右盼或交談等違規行為。

⑥ 意圖或已將試題紙或試題影音資料攜出或傳送出試場者，視同侵犯本中心著作財產權，限五年內不得報名參加「全民英檢」測驗。請人代考者，連同代考者，三年內不得報名參加本測驗。

⑦ 測驗結束時，須立即停止作答，在原位靜候監試人員收回全部試題紙且清點無誤，等候監試人員宣布結束後始可離場。

⑧ 入場、出場及測驗中如有違反上列規則或不服監試人員之指示者，監試人員將取消您的應試資格並請您離場，且作答不予計分，亦不退費。

請在 15 秒內完成並唸出下列自我介紹的句子：
My seat number is（座位號碼後 5 碼）, and my registration number is（准考證號碼後 5 碼）.

第一部分：朗讀短文 🔊 076

請先利用一分鐘的時間閱讀下面的短文，然後在二分鐘內以正常的速度，清楚正確的讀出下面的短文，閱讀時請不要發出聲音。

    I have to give a big presentation in class on Thursday. It's for history class, and it's about the civil war in the United States. This is a very interesting, emotional topic, and I have spent hours researching it online and in the library. My next task is to create a PowerPoint presentation that will impress my teacher as well as my fellow classmates. I will combine words and pictures to make it visually appealing. I am confident that I can get a good grade for this presentation.

*   *   *

    It is no secret that climate change is causing the world's oceans to become warmer. This threatens the existence of tiny corals, which live in shallow waters and form colorful coral reefs. Now, scientists are breeding corals that are better able to resist warmer ocean temperatures. They have achieved this through a process known as selective breeding. However, the scientists have warned that this alone will not protect corals in the future.

第二部分：回答問題 🔊 077-087

共十題。題目已事先錄音，每題經由耳機播出二次，不印在試卷上。第一至五題，每題回答時間 15 秒；第六至十題，每題回答時間 30 秒。每題播出後，請立即回答。回答時，不一定要用完整的句子，但請在作答時間內盡量的表達。

TEST 6

第三部分：看圖敘述 🔊 088

下面有一張圖片及四個相關的問題，請在一分半鐘內完成作答。作答時，請直接回答，不需將題號及題目唸出。

首先請利用 30 秒的時間看圖及問題。

❶ 這可能是什麼地方？
❷ 圖片中的這些人在做什麼？
❸ 你時常這麼做嗎？為什麼？
❹ 如果還有時間，請詳細描述圖片中的景物。

請將下列自我介紹的句子再唸一遍：

My seat number is （座位號碼後 5 碼）, and my registration number is （准考證號碼後 5 碼）.

GEPT 中級複試模擬測驗 第 ❼ 回
General English Proficiency Test — Intermediate Level Test 7

寫作能力測驗
- 第一部分：中譯英
- 第二部分：英文作文

口說能力測驗
- 第一部分：朗讀短文
- 第二部分：回答問題
- 第三部分：看圖敘述

寫作能力測驗

注意事項

① 本測驗共有兩部分。第一部分為中譯英，第二部分為英文作文。測驗時間為 **40 分鐘**。

② 請利用試題紙空白處及背面擬稿，但正答務必書寫在「寫作能力測驗答案紙」上。在答案紙以外的地方作答，不予計分。

③ 第一部分中譯英請在答案紙第一頁作答，第二部分英文作文請在答案紙第二頁作答。

④ 作答時請勿隔行書寫，請注意字跡應清晰可讀，並請保持答案紙之清潔，以免影響評分。

⑤ 測驗時，不得在准考證或其他物品上抄題，亦不得有傳遞、夾帶小抄、左顧右盼或交談等違規行為。

⑥ 意圖或已經將試卷攜出試場者，五年內不得報名參加本測驗。請人代考者，連同代考者，三年內不得報名參加本測驗。

⑦ 測驗結束時，須立即停止作答，在原位靜候監試人員收回全部試題紙及答案紙，清點無誤後，宣布結束始可離場。

⑧ 應試者入場、出場及測驗中如有違反上列規則或不服監試人員之指示者，監試人員得取消其應試資格並請其離場，且作答不予計分。

寫作能力測驗

本測驗共有兩部分。第一部分為中譯英，第二部分為英文作文。測驗時間為 **40 分鐘**。

第一部分：中譯英（40%）

說明：請將下列的一段中文翻譯成通順、達意且前後連貫的英文。

　　我向來都是個運動不行的人。我從來沒喜歡過學校的體育課，而且會刻意避免加入任何球隊。不過最近我發覺我很會跑。我跟幾個朋友在拼命跑要趕上捷運的末班車時，才意識到這個事實。我輕鬆趕上了車，但我的朋友全都沒趕上！這給了我自信，於是我就去練跑步。我現在每週跑三次，每次跑超過五公里。

第二部分：英文作文（60%）

說明：請依下面所提供的文字提示寫一篇英文作文，長度約 120 字（8 至 12 個句子）。作文可以是一個完整的段落，也可以分段。（評分重點包括內容、組織、文法、用字遣詞、標點符號、大小寫。）

提示：校園內的霸凌事件層出不窮，我們應該正視這個問題，讓校園成為學生快樂成長的地方。
　　　請寫一篇文章
　　❶ 你在學校曾遭遇過霸凌嗎？
　　❷ 你會怎麼解決校園內的霸凌問題？

TEST 7

本回完整音檔 🔊 007
本回分段音檔 🔊 089~101

口說能力測驗

注意事項

① 本測驗問題由耳機播放，回答則經麥克風錄下。分朗讀短文、回答問題與看圖敘述三部分，時間共約 15 分鐘，連同口試說明時間共需約五十分鐘。

② 第一部分朗讀短文有 1 分鐘準備時間，此時請勿唸出聲音，待聽到 "請開始朗讀" 2 分鐘的朗讀時間開始時，再將短文唸出來。第二部分回答問題的題目將播出二遍，聽完第二次題目後要立即回答。第三部分看圖敘述有 30 秒的思考時間及 1 分 30 秒的答題時間，思考時不可在試題紙上作記號，亦不可發出聲音。等聽到指示開始回答時，請您針對圖片在作答時間內盡量的回答。

③ 錄音設備皆已事先完成設定，請勿觸動任何機件，以免影響錄音。測驗時請戴妥耳機，將麥克風調到嘴邊約三公分處，聽清楚說明，依指示以適中音量回答。

④ 評分人員將根據您錄下的回答（發音與語調、語法與字彙、可解度及切題度等）作整體的評分。您可利用所附音檔自行測試，一一錄下回答後，再播出來聽聽，並斟酌調整。練習時請儘量以英語思考、應對，考試時較易有自然的表現。

⑤ 請注意測驗時不可在試題紙上劃線、打 "✓" 或作任何記號；不可在准考證或其他物品上抄題；亦不可有傳遞、夾帶小抄、左顧右盼或交談等違規行為。

⑥ 意圖或已將試題紙或試題影音資料攜出或傳送出試場者，視同侵犯本中心著作財產權，限五年內不得報名參加「全民英檢」測驗。請人代考者，連同代考者，三年內不得報名參加本測驗。

⑦ 測驗結束時，須立即停止作答，在原位靜候監試人員收回全部試題紙且清點無誤，等候監試人員宣布結束後始可離場。

⑧ 入場、出場及測驗中如有違反上列規則或不服監試人員之指示者，監試人員將取消您的應試資格並請您離場，且作答不予計分，亦不退費。

請在 **15** 秒內完成並唸出下列自我介紹的句子：
My seat number is（座位號碼後 5 碼）, and my registration number is（准考證號碼後 5 碼）.

第一部分：朗讀短文 🔊 089

請先利用一分鐘的時間閱讀下面的短文，然後在二分鐘內以正常的速度，清楚正確的讀出下面的短文，閱讀時請不要發出聲音。

Liam was looking forward to a trip to the skateboard park with his friends. When he set off from home, though, he noticed that his elderly neighbor, Rose, was working in her garden. She seemed to be tired and struggling with the manual work. Liam knew he must offer his assistance; the skateboarding could wait. Despite Rose's initial refusals, Liam took over the gardening and allowed his neighbor to rest. He was soon rewarded with a beaming smile and a glass of ice-cold lemonade.

✽　　　　　✽　　　　　✽

Western movies, which tell stories of life in the Old West of the US in the 19th century, often feature cowboys. However, the roots of the cowboy way of life stretch back as far as the 16th century. At this time, in what we now know as Mexico, Spanish colonists trained local men to ride horses and take care of cattle. As Spain expanded its empire across the southwestern part of North America, these cowboys did skillful and critical work that was also demanding and potentially dangerous.

第二部分：回答問題 🔊 090-100

共十題。題目已事先錄音，每題經由耳機播出二次，不印在試卷上。第一至五題，每題回答時間 15 秒；第六至十題，每題回答時間 30 秒。每題播出後，請立即回答。回答時，不一定要用完整的句子，但請在作答時間內盡量的表達。

TEST 7

第三部分：看圖敘述 🔊 101

下面有一張圖片及四個相關的問題，請在一分半鐘內完成作答。作答時，請直接回答，不需將題號及題目唸出。

首先請利用 30 秒的時間看圖及問題。

❶ 這可能是什麼地方？
❷ 圖片中的人在做什麼？
❸ 你時常從事這樣的休閒活動嗎？為什麼？
❹ 如果還有時間，請詳細描述圖片中的景物。

請將下列自我介紹的句子再唸一遍：

My seat number is ⟨座位號碼後 5 碼⟩, and my registration number is ⟨准考證號碼後 5 碼⟩.

GEPT 中級複試模擬測驗 第 8 回
General English Proficiency Test — Intermediate Level Test 8

寫作能力測驗
第一部分：中譯英
第二部分：英文作文

口說能力測驗
第一部分：朗讀短文
第二部分：回答問題
第三部分：看圖敘述

TEST 8

寫作能力測驗

注意事項

① 本測驗共有兩部分。第一部分為中譯英，第二部分為英文作文。測驗時間為 **40 分鐘**。

② 請利用試題紙空白處及背面擬稿，但正答務必書寫在「寫作能力測驗答案紙」上。在答案紙以外的地方作答，不予計分。

③ 第一部分中譯英請在答案紙第一頁作答，第二部分英文作文請在答案紙第二頁作答。

④ 作答時請勿隔行書寫，請注意字跡應清晰可讀，並請保持答案紙之清潔，以免影響評分。

⑤ 測驗時，不得在准考證或其他物品上抄題，亦不得有傳遞、夾帶小抄、左顧右盼或交談等違規行為。

⑥ 意圖或已經將試卷攜出試場者，五年內不得報名參加本測驗。請人代考者，連同代考者，三年內不得報名參加本測驗。

⑦ 測驗結束時，須立即停止作答，在原位靜候監試人員收回全部試題紙及答案紙，清點無誤後，宣布結束始可離場。

⑧ 應試者入場、出場及測驗中如有違反上列規則或不服監試人員之指示者，監試人員得取消其應試資格並請其離場，且作答不予計分。

本測驗共有兩部分。第一部分為中譯英，第二部分為英文作文。測驗時間為 **40 分鐘**。

第一部分：中譯英（40%）

說明：請將下列的一段中文翻譯成通順、達意且前後連貫的英文。

　　我哥哥喬許（Josh）說他想在他生日那天早起看日出。我問他為什麼會有這種願望，他回答說他向來都睡很晚，從沒看過日出。於是在他生日當天，我們起了個大早，然後踏上通往公寓大樓屋頂的樓梯。我起初感到有點煩又很想睡覺，但當我看到喬許看著日出時臉上充滿了喜悅之情時，這些負面情緒就逐漸消失了。這是我與哥哥共享的美好時刻。

第二部分：英文作文（60%）

說明：請依下面所提供的文字提示寫一篇英文作文，長度約 120 字（8 至 12 個句子）。作文可以是一個完整的段落，也可以分段。（評分重點包括內容、組織、文法、用字遣詞、標點符號、大小寫。）

提示：西諺有云：「滾石不生苔。」我們要時時保有求知慾、挑戰自己，讓自己去學習不同的新事物。請寫一篇文章
　　❶ 請講述一個你嘗試新事物的時機點
　　❷ 你學到了什麼？

TEST 8

本回完整音檔 🔊 008
本回分段音檔 🔊 102~114

口說能力測驗

注意事項

① 本測驗問題由耳機播放，回答則經麥克風錄下。分朗讀短文、回答問題與看圖敘述三部分，時間共約 15 分鐘，連同口試說明時間共需約五十分鐘。

② 第一部分朗讀短文有 1 分鐘準備時間，此時請勿唸出聲音，待聽到"請開始朗讀" 2 分鐘的朗讀時間開始時，再將短文唸出來。第二部分回答問題的題目將播出二遍，聽完第二次題目後要立即回答。第三部分看圖敘述有 30 秒的思考時間及 1 分 30 秒的答題時間，思考時不可在試題紙上作記號，亦不可發出聲音。等聽到指示開始回答時，請您針對圖片在作答時間內盡量的回答。

③ 錄音設備皆已事先完成設定，請勿觸動任何機件，以免影響錄音。測驗時請戴妥耳機，將麥克風調到嘴邊約三公分處，聽清楚說明，依指示以適中音量回答。

④ 評分人員將根據您錄下的回答（發音與語調、語法與字彙、可解度及切題度等）作整體的評分。您可利用所附音檔自行測試，一一錄下回答後，再播出來聽聽，並斟酌調整。練習時請儘量以英語思考、應對，考試時較易有自然的表現。

⑤ 請注意測驗時不可在試題紙上劃線、打"✓"或作任何記號；不可在准考證或其他物品上抄題；亦不可有傳遞、夾帶小抄、左顧右盼或交談等違規行為。

⑥ 意圖或已將試題紙或試題影音資料攜出或傳送出試場者，視同侵犯本中心著作財產權，限五年內不得報名參加「全民英檢」測驗。請人代考者，連同代考者，三年內不得報名參加本測驗。

⑦ 測驗結束時，須立即停止作答，在原位靜候監試人員收回全部試題紙且清點無誤，等候監試人員宣布結束後始可離場。

⑧ 入場、出場及測驗中如有違反上列規則或不服監試人員之指示者，監試人員將取消您的應試資格並請您離場，且作答不予計分，亦不退費。

請在 **15** 秒內完成並唸出下列自我介紹的句子：
My seat number is（座位號碼後 5 碼）, and my registration number is（准考證號碼後 5 碼）.

第一部分：朗讀短文 🔊 102

請先利用一分鐘的時間閱讀下面的短文，然後在二分鐘內以正常的速度，清楚正確的讀出下面的短文，閱讀時請不要發出聲音。

  Rodney is from the US. His first visit to Taiwan was defined by friendly people, delicious food, and world-class public transportation. However, Rodney also experienced some culture shock. He was surprised by the number of scooters that were parked on sidewalks. He was astonished by the sight of women carrying umbrellas to block out the sun. He was amazed that he didn't need to tip in any of the restaurants. And he was shocked to see so many people standing on only one side of the escalators!

    ＊   ＊   ＊

  Nowadays, people lead very busy lives, and many struggle to fit a workout such as a long run or a swimming session into their daily schedule. However, recent research has shown that adding short bursts of exercise into our day can be just as beneficial for our physical and mental health. These "exercise snacks" can be as simple as ascending a few flights of stairs, taking a short, fast walk during lunchtime, or performing a few squats at your office desk.

第二部分：回答問題 🔊 103-113

共十題。題目已事先錄音，每題經由耳機播出二次，不印在試卷上。第一至五題，每題回答時間 15 秒；第六至十題，每題回答時間 30 秒。每題播出後，請立即回答。回答時，不一定要用完整的句子，但請在作答時間內盡量的表達。

TEST 8

第三部分：看圖敘述 🔊 114

下面有一張圖片及四個相關的問題，請在一分半鐘內完成作答。作答時，請直接回答，不需將題號及題目唸出。

首先請利用 30 秒的時間看圖及問題。

❶ 這可能是什麼地方？
❷ 圖片中的這些人在做什麼？
❸ 這樣很重要嗎？為什麼？你也會這麼做嗎？
❹ 如果還有時間，請詳細描述圖片中的景物。

請將下列自我介紹的句子再唸一遍：

My seat number is（座位號碼後 5 碼）, and my registration number is（准考證號碼後 5 碼）.

GEPT 中級複試模擬測驗 第 ❾ 回
General English Proficiency Test — Intermediate Level Test 9

寫作能力測驗
第一部分：中譯英
第二部分：英文作文

口說能力測驗
第一部分：朗讀短文
第二部分：回答問題
第三部分：看圖敘述

寫作能力測驗

注意事項

① 本測驗共有兩部分。第一部分為中譯英,第二部分為英文作文。測驗時間為 **40 分鐘**。

② 請利用試題紙空白處及背面擬稿,但正答務必書寫在「寫作能力測驗答案紙」上。在答案紙以外的地方作答,不予計分。

③ 第一部分中譯英請在答案紙第一頁作答,第二部分英文作文請在答案紙第二頁作答。

④ 作答時請勿隔行書寫,請注意字跡應清晰可讀,並請保持答案紙之清潔,以免影響評分。

⑤ 測驗時,不得在准考證或其他物品上抄題,亦不得有傳遞、夾帶小抄、左顧右盼或交談等違規行為。

⑥ 意圖或已經將試卷攜出試場者,五年內不得報名參加本測驗。請人代考者,連同代考者,三年內不得報名參加本測驗。

⑦ 測驗結束時,須立即停止作答,在原位靜候監試人員收回全部試題紙及答案紙,清點無誤後,宣布結束始可離場。

⑧ 應試者入場、出場及測驗中如有違反上列規則或不服監試人員之指示者,監試人員得取消其應試資格並請其離場,且作答不予計分。

寫作能力測驗

本測驗共有兩部分。第一部分為中譯英，第二部分為英文作文。測驗時間為 **40 分鐘**。

第一部分：中譯英（40%）

說明：請將下列的一段中文翻譯成通順、達意且前後連貫的英文。

　　亞伯特（Albert）覺得自己平日的穿著打扮有點乏味，於是決定改變造型。他跑去理髮店要求剪個新髮型，於是理髮師剃掉了亞伯特腦後與兩側的頭髮。亞伯特又選擇剃掉他留了十年的絡腮鬍，改成八字鬍。然後他跑去一間服飾店，買了各式各樣的潮服與配飾。看來亞伯特是鐵了心要改變他的外貌了。

第二部分：英文作文（60%）

說明：請依下面所提供的文字提示寫一篇英文作文，長度約 120 字（8 至 12 個句子）。作文可以是一個完整的段落，也可以分段。（評分重點包括內容、組織、文法、用字遣詞、標點符號、大小寫。）

提示：許多人在求學階段，最後往往會選擇就讀大學，以期望有更好的未來與就業機會。請寫一篇文章

❶ 請問你覺得讀大學的好處在哪裡？

❷ 你覺得每個人都應該可以免費上大學嗎？為什麼？

TEST 9

本回完整音檔 ◀)) 009
本回分段音檔 ◀)) 115~127

口說能力測驗

注意事項

① 本測驗問題由耳機播放，回答則經麥克風錄下。分朗讀短文、回答問題與看圖敘述三部分，時間共約 15 分鐘，連同口試說明時間共需約五十分鐘。

② 第一部分朗讀短文有 1 分鐘準備時間，此時請勿唸出聲音，待聽到"請開始朗讀" 2 分鐘的朗讀時間開始時，再將短文唸出來。第二部分回答問題的題目將播出二遍，聽完第二次題目後要立即回答。第三部分看圖敘述有 30 秒的思考時間及 1 分 30 秒的答題時間，思考時不可在試題紙上作記號，亦不可發出聲音。等聽到指示開始回答時，請您針對圖片在作答時間內盡量的回答。

③ 錄音設備皆已事先完成設定，請勿觸動任何機件，以免影響錄音。測驗時請戴妥耳機，將麥克風調到嘴邊約三公分處，聽清楚說明，依指示以適中音量回答。

④ 評分人員將根據您錄下的回答（發音與語調、語法與字彙、可解度及切題度等）作整體的評分。您可利用所附音檔自行測試，一一錄下回答後，再播出來聽聽，並斟酌調整。練習時請儘量以英語思考、應對，考試時較易有自然的表現。

⑤ 請注意測驗時不可在試題紙上劃線、打"✓"或作任何記號；不可在准考證或其他物品上抄題；亦不可有傳遞、夾帶小抄、左顧右盼或交談等違規行為。

⑥ 意圖或已將試題紙或試題影音資料攜出或傳送出試場者，視同侵犯本中心著作財產權，限五年內不得報名參加「全民英檢」測驗。請人代考者，連同代考者，三年內不得報名參加本測驗。

⑦ 測驗結束時，須立即停止作答，在原位靜候監試人員收回全部試題紙且清點無誤，等候監試人員宣布結束後始可離場。

⑧ 入場、出場及測驗中如有違反上列規則或不服監試人員之指示者，監試人員將取消您的應試資格並請您離場，且作答不予計分，亦不退費。

請在 15 秒內完成並唸出下列自我介紹的句子：
My seat number is（座位號碼後 5 碼）, and my registration number is（准考證號碼後 5 碼）.

第一部分：朗讀短文 🔊 115

請先利用一分鐘的時間閱讀下面的短文，然後在二分鐘內以正常的速度，清楚正確的讀出下面的短文，閱讀時請不要發出聲音。

Tara loves reading novels, but she thinks that new books are too expensive. Therefore, she visits lots of second-hand bookstores to see if she can discover any novels that appeal to her. She found one the other day in a bookstore down an alley near her mom's office. The book was a fantasy romance. This wouldn't normally be Tara's cup of tea, but the reviews shown on the cover were so positive that she thought she should give it a shot.

❋   ❋   ❋

Bonsai trees are tiny trees that are grown in pots. They are intended to resemble full-size trees and are carefully cultivated over years or even decades. This is achieved through cutting roots, using wires to direct branch growth, and changing pots every few years. The art of bonsai is primarily associated with Japan, where the skills of patience, imagination, and devotion required for the practice are highly regarded. It can be considered a perfect example of the harmony between humans and nature.

第二部分：回答問題 🔊 116-126

共十題。題目已事先錄音，每題經由耳機播出二次，不印在試卷上。第一至五題，每題回答時間 15 秒；第六至十題，每題回答時間 30 秒。每題播出後，請立即回答。回答時，不一定要用完整的句子，但請在作答時間內盡量的表達。

TEST 9

第三部分：看圖敘述 🔊 127

下面有一張圖片及四個相關的問題，請在一分半鐘內完成作答。作答時，請直接回答，不需將題號及題目唸出。

首先請利用 30 秒的時間看圖及問題。

❶ 這可能是什麼地方？
❷ 圖片中的是什麼人，他們在做什麼？
❸ 你會想要嘗試相同的工作嗎？為什麼？
❹ 如果還有時間，請詳細描述圖片中的景物。

請將下列自我介紹的句子再唸一遍：

My seat number is (座位號碼後 5 碼), and my registration number is (准考證號碼後 5 碼).

GEPT 中級複試模擬測驗　第 ❿ 回
General English Proficiency Test — Intermediate Level Test 10

寫作能力測驗
第一部分：中譯英
第二部分：英文作文

口說能力測驗
第一部分：朗讀短文
第二部分：回答問題
第三部分：看圖敘述

寫作能力測驗

注意事項

① 本測驗共有兩部分。第一部分為中譯英，第二部分為英文作文。測驗時間為 **40 分鐘**。

② 請利用試題紙空白處及背面擬稿，但正答務必書寫在「寫作能力測驗答案紙」上。在答案紙以外的地方作答，不予計分。

③ 第一部分中譯英請在答案紙第一頁作答，第二部分英文作文請在答案紙第二頁作答。

④ 作答時請勿隔行書寫，請注意字跡應清晰可讀，並請保持答案紙之清潔，以免影響評分。

⑤ 測驗時，不得在准考證或其他物品上抄題，亦不得有傳遞、夾帶小抄、左顧右盼或交談等違規行為。

⑥ 意圖或已經將試卷攜出試場者，五年內不得報名參加本測驗。請人代考者，連同代考者，三年內不得報名參加本測驗。

⑦ 測驗結束時，須立即停止作答，在原位靜候監試人員收回全部試題紙及答案紙，清點無誤後，宣布結束始可離場。

⑧ 應試者入場、出場及測驗中如有違反上列規則或不服監試人員之指示者，監試人員得取消其應試資格並請其離場，且作答不予計分。

本測驗共有兩部分。第一部分為中譯英，第二部分為英文作文。測驗時間為 **40 分鐘**。

第一部分：中譯英（40%）

說明：請將下列的一段中文翻譯成通順、達意且前後連貫的英文。

　　希臘是以歷史遺跡聞名的國家。所以當莎夏（Sasha）去那裡時，想要盡可能看到越多遺跡越好。在首都市區內，她造訪了山丘上的若干座古代建築物，其中一座是祭拜某位女神的神廟。她也跑去參觀了一個市集的遺跡，古代的人們會在那裡交易商品與觀看表演。莎夏對於所看到的一切都感到不可思議，決定未來還要再造訪這片土地。

第二部分：英文作文（60%）

說明：請依下面所提供的文字提示寫一篇英文作文，長度約 120 字（8 至 12 個句子）。作文可以是一個完整的段落，也可以分段。（評分重點包括內容、組織、文法、用字遣詞、標點符號、大小寫。）

提示：許多人長大後才有機會開始理財，而理財不單單只是儲蓄而已，還包含投資與預算規畫等等，我們從小就應該開始培養正確的理財觀念。請寫一篇文章
① 你認為學校應該教育學生如何理財嗎？
② 請說明原因

TEST 10

本回完整音檔 🔊 010
本回分段音檔 🔊 128~140

口說能力測驗

注意事項

① 本測驗問題由耳機播放，回答則經麥克風錄下。分朗讀短文、回答問題與看圖敘述三部分，時間共約 15 分鐘，連同口試說明時間共需約五十分鐘。

② 第一部分朗讀短文有 1 分鐘準備時間，此時請勿唸出聲音，待聽到 "請開始朗讀" 2 分鐘的朗讀時間開始時，再將短文唸出來。第二部分回答問題的題目將播出二遍，聽完第二次題目後要立即回答。第三部分看圖敘述有 30 秒的思考時間及 1 分 30 秒的答題時間，思考時不可在試題紙上作記號，亦不可發出聲音。等聽到指示開始回答時，請您針對圖片在作答時間內盡量的回答。

③ 錄音設備皆已事先完成設定，請勿觸動任何機件，以免影響錄音。測驗時請戴妥耳機，將麥克風調到嘴邊約三公分處，聽清楚說明，依指示以適中音量回答。

④ 評分人員將根據您錄下的回答（發音與語調、語法與字彙、可解度及切題度等）作整體的評分。您可利用所附音檔自行測試，一一錄下回答後，再播出來聽聽，並斟酌調整。練習時請儘量以英語思考、應對，考試時較易有自然的表現。

⑤ 請注意測驗時不可在試題紙上劃線、打 "✓" 或作任何記號；不可在准考證或其他物品上抄題；亦不可有傳遞、夾帶小抄、左顧右盼或交談等違規行為。

⑥ 意圖或已將試題紙或試題影音資料攜出或傳送出試場者，視同侵犯本中心著作財產權，限五年內不得報名參加「全民英檢」測驗。請人代考者，連同代考者，三年內不得報名參加本測驗。

⑦ 測驗結束時，須立即停止作答，在原位靜候監試人員收回全部試題紙且清點無誤，等候監試人員宣布結束後始可離場。

⑧ 入場、出場及測驗中如有違反上列規則或不服監試人員之指示者，監試人員將取消您的應試資格並請您離場，且作答不予計分，亦不退費。

請在 15 秒內完成並唸出下列自我介紹的句子：
My seat number is（座位號碼後 5 碼）, and my registration number is（准考證號碼後 5 碼）.

第一部分：朗讀短文　🔊 128

請先利用一分鐘的時間閱讀下面的短文，然後在二分鐘內以正常的速度，清楚正確的讀出下面的短文，閱讀時請不要發出聲音。

　　When Benny was 14, his parents considered him mature and capable enough to look after his younger sibling on his own. One night when they went out for a meal, they left Benny in charge of watching his sister, Diana. Benny felt a little anxious, but he rose to the occasion. He played games with Diana, gave her something to eat, made sure she had a bath and brushed her teeth, and then put her to bed. His parents were very proud of him.

＊　　　　＊　　　　＊

　　Extreme heat events are on the rise around the globe, and they have the potential to kill. That is because when we're exposed to high temperatures for a long time, our body must work harder to cool down. We start to sweat, which can lead to dehydration if we don't drink sufficient water. This causes our heart to pump harder and can result in heat exhaustion, dizziness, and confusion. If our body temperature rises past 40°C, we can develop heatstroke, which is a medical emergency.

第二部分：回答問題　🔊 129-139

共十題。題目已事先錄音，每題經由耳機播出二次，不印在試卷上。第一至五題，每題回答時間 15 秒；第六至十題，每題回答時間 30 秒。每題播出後，請立即回答。回答時，不一定要用完整的句子，但請在作答時間內盡量的表達。

TEST 10

第三部分：看圖敘述 🔊 140

下面有一張圖片及四個相關的問題，請在一分半鐘內完成作答。作答時，請直接回答，不需將題號及題目唸出。

首先請利用 30 秒的時間看圖及問題。

❶ 這可能是什麼地方？
❷ 圖片中的人在做什麼？她為什麼這麼做？
❸ 你認為這麼做好嗎？
❹ 如果還有時間，請詳細描述圖片中的景物。

請將下列自我介紹的句子再唸一遍：

My seat number is （座位號碼後 5 碼）, and my registration number is （准考證號碼後 5 碼）.

NOTES

NOTES

NOTES

NOTES

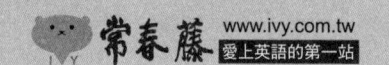

GEPT 附錄：測驗用答案紙
General English Proficiency Test—Intermediate Level Test

中級

GEPT 全民英語能力分級檢定測驗
常春藤全民英檢 中級 寫作能力測驗答案紙 第 1 回

座位號碼： 561-01-01121　　　　　　　試卷別：＿＿＿＿＿＿＿

第一部分：中譯英（40%），請由第 1 行開始並於框線內作答，勿隔行書寫。

（第二部分：英文作文，請翻至背面作答。）

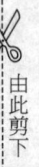

GEPT 全民英語能力分級檢定測驗

常春藤全民英檢 　**中級** 寫作能力測驗答案紙　**第 2 回**

座位號碼：　561-01-01121　　　　　　　　試卷別：＿＿＿＿＿＿＿

第一部分：中譯英（40%），請由第 1 行開始並於<u>框線內</u>作答，勿隔行書寫。

1

5

10

15

（第二部分：英文作文，請翻至背面作答。）

第 1 頁

座位號碼：561-01-01121
第二部分：英文作文（60%），請由第 1 行開始並於框線內作答，勿隔行書寫。

GEPT 全民英語能力分級檢定測驗
常春藤全民英檢 中級 寫作能力測驗答案紙 第 3 回

座位號碼：　561-01-01121　　　　　　試卷別：_____

第一部分：中譯英（40%），請由第 1 行開始並於框線內作答，勿隔行書寫。

（第二部分：英文作文，請翻至背面作答。）

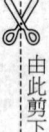

GEPT 全民英語能力分級檢定測驗
常春藤全民英檢 中級 寫作能力測驗答案紙 第 **4** 回

座位號碼： 561-01-01121　　　　　　　試卷別：＿＿＿＿＿＿＿

第一部分：中譯英（40%），請由第 1 行開始並於框線內作答，勿隔行書寫。

（第二部分：英文作文，請翻至背面作答。）

GEPT 全民英語能力分級檢定測驗
常春藤全民英檢 中級 寫作能力測驗答案紙 第 5 回

座位號碼： 561-01-01121   試卷別：＿＿＿＿＿＿＿

第一部分：中譯英（40%），請由第 1 行開始並於框線內作答，勿隔行書寫。

（第二部分：英文作文，請翻至背面作答。）

GEPT 全民英語能力分級檢定測驗

常春藤全民英檢　　中級 寫作能力測驗答案紙　第 6 回

座位號碼：　561-01-01121　　　　　試卷別：＿＿＿＿＿＿＿＿

第一部分：中譯英（40%），請由第 1 行開始並於框線內作答，勿隔行書寫。

（第二部分：英文作文，請翻至背面作答。）

GEPT 全民英語能力分級檢定測驗

常春藤全民英檢

中級 寫作能力測驗答案紙 第 7 回

座位號碼： 561-01-01121　　　　試卷別：

第一部分：中譯英（40%），請由第 1 行開始並於框線內作答，勿隔行書寫。

由此剪下

由此剪下

（第二部分：英文作文，請翻至背面作答。）

座位號碼：561-01-01121
第二部分：英文作文（60%），請由第 1 行開始並於框線內作答，勿隔行書寫。

GEPT 全民英語能力分級檢定測驗
常春藤全民英檢　中級 寫作能力測驗答案紙　第 8 回

座位號碼：　561-01-01121　　　　　試卷別：_____

第一部分：中譯英（40%），請由第 1 行開始並於框線內作答，勿隔行書寫。

1
_____
_____
_____
_____
5 _____
_____
_____
_____
_____
10 _____
_____
_____
_____
_____
15 _____

（第二部分：英文作文，請翻至背面作答。）

座位號碼：561-01-01121

第二部分：英文作文（60%），請由第 1 行開始並於框線內作答，勿隔行書寫。

GEPT 全民英語能力分級檢定測驗
常春藤全民英檢 中級 寫作能力測驗答案紙 第 9 回

座位號碼： 561-01-01121　　　　　試卷別：＿＿＿＿＿＿＿

第一部分：中譯英（40%），請由第 1 行開始並於框線內作答，勿隔行書寫。

（第二部分：英文作文，請翻至背面作答。）

第 1 頁

座位號碼：561-01-01121

第二部分：英文作文（60%），請由第 1 行開始並於框線內作答，勿隔行書寫。

GEPT 全民英語能力分級檢定測驗

常春藤全民英檢 中級 寫作能力測驗答案紙 第10回

座位號碼： 561-01-01121　　　　　　　試卷別：＿＿＿＿＿＿＿＿

第一部分：中譯英（40%），請由第 1 行開始並於框線內作答，勿隔行書寫。

（第二部分：英文作文，請翻至背面作答。）

第 1 頁

常春藤全民英檢系列【G68-1】
準！GEPT 全民英檢中級複試 10 回高分模擬試題＋翻譯解答（寫作＆口說）－試題本

總 編 審	賴世雄
終 審	梁民康
執行編輯	許嘉華
編輯小組	常春藤中外編輯群
設計組長	王玥琦
封面設計	林桂旭・王穎緁
排版設計	林桂旭・王穎緁
錄 音	劉書吟
播音老師	Karen Chen・Jacob Roth
法律顧問	北辰著作權事務所蕭雄淋律師
出 版 者	常春藤數位出版股份有限公司
地 址	臺北市忠孝西路一段 33 號 5 樓
電 話	(02) 2331-7600
傳 真	(02) 2381-0918
網 址	www.ivy.com.tw
電子信箱	service@ivy.com.tw
郵政劃撥	50463568
戶 名	常春藤數位出版股份有限公司
定 價	230 元（2 書＋音檔）

©常春藤數位出版股份有限公司 (2025) All rights reserved.　　Y000042-3577
本書之封面、內文、編排等之著作財產權歸常春藤數位出版股份有限公司所有。未經本公司書面同意，請勿翻印、轉載或為一切著作權法上利用行為，否則依法追究。

如有缺頁、裝訂錯誤或破損，請寄回本公司更換。　　【版權所有　翻印必究】

準 全新撰寫！
題目精準、刷題有感，考生一致推薦！

GEPT
全民英檢
中級複試 10回
高分模擬試題＋翻譯解答
寫作＆口說

【翻譯解答本】

Contents
目 錄

Test ❶
寫作能力測驗 1
口說能力測驗 🔊 141-143 2

Test ❷
寫作能力測驗 9
口說能力測驗 🔊 144-146 10

Test ❸
寫作能力測驗 17
口說能力測驗 🔊 147-149 18

Test ❹
寫作能力測驗 24
口說能力測驗 🔊 150-152 25

Test ❺
寫作能力測驗 32
口說能力測驗 🔊 153-155 33

Test ❻
寫作能力測驗 39
口說能力測驗 🔊 156-158 40

Test ❼
寫作能力測驗 46
口說能力測驗 🔊 159-161 47

Test ❽
寫作能力測驗 54
口說能力測驗 🔊 162-164 54

Test ❾
寫作能力測驗 61
口說能力測驗 🔊 165-167 62

Test ❿
寫作能力測驗 68
口說能力測驗 🔊 168-170 69

GEPT 中級複試模擬測驗 第 ❶ 回　參考解答與翻譯

寫作能力測驗

◉ 第一部分：中譯英

氣象預報說週末是好天氣，所以爸爸建議全家人利用這機會去山上露營。我們把帳篷塞進大包包裡，然後開車到老爸在網路上訂好的營地。那裡的景色非常壯觀。我們把帳篷搭起來，然後爸爸做了一頓簡單的晚飯，但卻非常好吃。晚上我們圍坐在營火旁觀賞晴朗夜空中的流星。這真是一次令人難忘的露營之旅。

參考解答

The forecasters said the weather would be nice over the weekend, so Dad suggested that the whole family take the opportunity to go camping in the mountains. We stuffed the tents in huge bags and drove to the campsite Dad had booked online. The view from up there was amazing. We pitched our tents, and Dad made a simple yet delicious meal. At nighttime, we sat around the campfire and watched the shooting stars in the clear sky. It was definitely a camping trip to remember.

重要單字片語

- **forecaster** [ˈfɔr͵kæstɚ] *n.* 氣象預報員
= weather forecaster
例 The forecaster said we are going to have snowstorms tomorrow.
氣象報告說明天會有暴風雪。

- **stuff** [stʌf] *vt.* 塞滿
例 This closet is stuffed with clothes I don't wear anymore.
這個衣櫥塞滿我再也不穿的衣服。

- **pitch** [pɪtʃ] *vt.* 紮（營）
例 Let's pitch our tent by the river.
咱們在河邊紮營吧。

◉ 第二部分：英文作文

當我們在發育時，最需要的就是吃得健康、吃得營養。尤其是在求學階段，我們更需要關注學校所提供的餐點。請寫一篇文章

❶ 請問你在學校吃的是健康的餐點嗎？
❷ 學校該如何鼓勵學生吃得健康？

參考解答

Most of the meals that I have at school are quite healthy. They typically contain lots of vegetables, including carrots, cabbage, and broccoli, and good-quality protein such as fish, eggs, and tofu. We are usually given lots of fruit, too. However, the lunches sometimes include less healthy options like fried chicken, hamburgers, and overly processed food such as sausages.

The best way for schools to promote healthy eating is to teach their students about the benefits of a balanced diet. They should tell them how important it is to eat a variety of freshly cooked ingredients. They should educate them about the dangers of consuming too much salt and fat, and they should discuss the need to monitor our sugar intake.

我在學校吃到的餐點大部分都相當健康，通常會有許多蔬菜，包括紅蘿蔔、高麗菜、綠花椰菜，以及優質蛋白質如魚、蛋、豆腐等。我們也常吃到許多水果。不過午餐偶而會有不那麼健康的食物，像是炸雞、漢堡，或像是香腸等過度加工的食物。

學校鼓勵吃得健康的最佳辦法，是教導學生均衡飲食的益處。他們應該告訴學生吃到各種新鮮烹煮食材的重要性。他們應該教育學生吃太鹹太油的危險，也該提到控制糖分攝取量的必要性。

TEST 1

TEST 1

重要單字片語

- **contain** [kənˋten] *vt.* 包含
- 例 Try to avoid foods that contain a lot of fat.
  儘量避免吃含有過多脂肪的食物。
- **broccoli** [ˋbrɑkəlɪ] *n.* 綠花椰菜
- **protein** [ˋprotiɪn] *n.* 蛋白質
- **processed** [ˋprɑsɛst] *a.* 加工的
  processed foods　　加工食品
- **educate** [ˋɛdʒə͵ket] *vt.* 教育
- 例 Bill and his wife are constantly arguing over how to educate their children.
  比爾和他太太針對如何教育孩子一事經常發生爭執。
- **intake** [ˋɪn͵tek] *n.* 攝取量

口說能力測驗

第一部分：朗讀短文　　141

I usually get a ride to school, so I rarely need to take the bus. This morning, though, my regular ride wasn't available. Therefore, I had to take public transportation during rush hour. It felt like there were thousands of people on my bus, and we were all crammed together. The traffic was awful, too, so the journey seemed to take forever. To make matters worse, it was raining, so everyone was carrying wet umbrellas. I hope my ride is available tomorrow!

我通常都是坐別人的車上學，所以很少需要搭公車。但今天早上人家沒法載我，所以我不得不在尖峰時間搭乘大眾交通。我搭的公車上感覺好像站了成千上萬人，所有人都是臉貼臉、背貼背。路上也很塞，所以這趟車好像要搭到天長地久的感覺。更討厭的是外面在下雨，所以每個人都拿著一把溼雨傘。希望明天載我的人會有空！

重要單字片語

- **ride** [raɪd] *n.* 搭便車；乘坐
- **regular** [ˋrɛɡjələ] *a.* 經常發生的；規律的
- **available** [əˋveləbḷ] *a.* 可用的，可得到的
- **transportation** [͵trænspɚˋteʃən] *n.* 交通運輸（工具）（不可數）
- **rush hour**　　尖峰時刻
- **cram** [kræm] *vt.* 硬塞
- 例 Sam crammed his school books into a small backpack and went home.
  山姆把課本都塞進一個小背包，然後回家了。
- **take forever**　　耗時很久

As many countries try to reduce their dependence on fossil fuels, they are using more and more renewable energy sources. Two common sources are solar and wind power. Solar energy involves using the sunlight to create electricity through solar panels. This type of energy is clean, but it relies heavily on sunny weather. Wind energy, on the other hand, uses wind turbines to change the power of the wind into electricity. It, too, is dependent on the weather, and some people find wind turbines noisy and ugly.

由於許多國家都想降低對化石燃料的依賴，因此使用越來越多再生能源。太陽能與風能就是兩種常見的再生能源。太陽能是利用太陽光，經由太陽能板來發電。這種能源乾淨歸乾淨，但卻極度依賴有太陽的天氣。而風能是利用風力渦輪機將風力轉換成電力。風能也得看天吃飯，而且有些人覺得渦輪機很吵又有礙觀瞻。

重要單字片語

- **reduce** [rɪˋdjus] *vt.* 使減少
  reduce pollution　　減少汙染

- **fossil** [ˈfɑsl̩] *n.* 化石 & *a.* 化石的
  fossil fuel [ˈfɑsl̩ ˌfjuəl]
  化石燃料（如石油、煤、天然氣等）
- **renewable** [rɪˈnjuəbl̩] *a.* （能源）可再生的
  renewable energy [rɪˈnjuəbl̩ ˈɛnədʒɪ] *n.*
  再生能源
- **solar** [ˈsolɚ] *a.* 太陽的；與太陽有關的
- **electricity** [ɪˌlɛkˈtrɪsətɪ] *n.* 電；電力
- **panel** [ˈpænl̩] *n.* 嵌版；儀表板
- **turbine** [ˈtɝbaɪn] *n.* 渦輪機

◉ 第二部分：回答問題　🔊 142

❶ If you were struggling to concentrate on a task, what would you do?
如果你沒法專注在某件工作上時，你會怎麼辦？

示範回答

① I would go and make myself a cup of coffee. Taking a break and consuming some caffeine always helps me to focus on what I'm doing.
我會去泡杯咖啡。休息一下來一點咖啡因，總能幫我專注在當下的工作之上。

② If I couldn't concentrate on a task, I would go for a walk in the fresh air. This has been proven to help you re-focus.
如果我沒辦法專心工作，就會去散個步呼吸一點新鮮空氣。這已經證實可以幫人找回專注。

重要單字片語

- **concentrate** [ˈkɑnsn̩ˌtret] *vt.* & *vi.* 集中
  concentrate on... 　專注於……
  = focus on...
- **caffeine** [kæˈfin] *n.* 咖啡因

❷ Do you enjoy eating great food? What is the best meal that you have ever eaten?
你喜歡美食嗎？你吃過最棒的一頓飯有什麼菜色？

示範回答

① Yes, I do! The best meal I have ever had was in Kobe in Japan. The beef there was so delicious. I'll remember that meal for the rest of my life.
我喜歡美食！我吃過最棒的一餐是在日本的神戶。那裡的牛肉好吃極了。我一輩子都忘不了那一餐。

② I get to eat the best meal of my life every Sunday! That's when my grandma makes food for the whole family. Nothing beats the taste or variety of her cooking.
我每個星期天都吃到人生最棒的一頓飯！我阿嬤在那天會做飯給全家人吃。她做的菜的味道跟花樣變化都是無人能敵。

❸ Would you like to own an electric car? Why or why not?
你想要擁有電動汽車嗎？請說明理由。

示範回答

① Yes, I would love to own one. They're much better for the environment than regular cars, so I could make my contribution to reducing climate change.
我很想要電動車。電動汽車比一般車子更環境友善，這樣我就算是為減緩氣候變遷盡了一份心力。

② No, electric cars don't interest me at all. For one thing, they're too expensive. For another, you have to charge them, which is troublesome.
不想。我對電動汽車一點興趣都沒有。第一，它太貴了。第二，你還要給它們充電，很麻煩。

TEST 1

3

TEST 1

重要單字片語

- **electric** [ɪˈlɛktrɪk] *a.* 電的
  an electric light / car / blanket
  電燈 / 電動汽車 / 電熱毯
- **regular** [ˈrɛgjələ] *a.* 普通的，一般的
- **contribution** [ˌkɑntrəˈbjuʃən] *n.* 貢獻；捐獻
  make a contribution to N/V-ing
  對……貢獻
  例 Frank was rewarded for making a major contribution to the company.
  法蘭克因對公司有重大貢獻而獲得獎勵。
- **interest** [ˈɪnt(ə)rɪst] *vt.* 使……感興趣
  例 The novel interested me a lot. I want to read it again.
  我對那本小說很感興趣。我想要再讀一遍。
- **charge** [tʃɑrdʒ] *vt. & vi.* 充電；收費

❹ Your friend is moving from the city to the countryside. What would you say to him?
你的朋友要從市區搬家到鄉下。你會跟他說什麼？

示範回答

① I'd congratulate him and tell him that I'm jealous! I'd say that living in the fresh air in a rural area will be great for his health.
我會恭喜他並且說我很嫉妒他！我會說住在空氣新鮮的鄉村地區對他的健康很好。

② I'd ask him if he has thought the decision through. Does he really want to leave the convenience and excitement of city life behind?
我會問他有沒有好好想過這個決定。他是否真的想把城市生活的便利與刺激統統拋諸腦後嗎？

重要單字片語

- **countryside** [ˈkʌntrɪˌsaɪd] *n.* 鄉間（不可數）
- **congratulate** [kənˈgrætʃəˌlet] *vt.* 道賀，慶賀
  congratulate sb on sth 就某事恭賀某人
  例 Let's congratulate the boss on his engagement.
  老闆訂婚了，我們去道賀吧。
- **jealous** [ˈdʒɛləs] *a.* 嫉妒的，吃醋的
- **rural** [ˈrʊrəl] *a.* 鄉下的
  a rural area 鄉村地區

❺ How important do you think table manners are in today's world?
你認為在現在的社會裡，餐桌禮儀有多重要？

示範回答

① I think they're very important because we should show respect to our fellow diners. For example, we shouldn't talk with our mouth full of food because it's rude.
我覺得餐桌禮儀很重要，因為我們應該尊重同桌用餐的人。例如滿嘴食物時不要說話，因為那樣很沒禮貌。

② There are more important things in the world than table manners. I don't think using the wrong silverware or burping occasionally is such a big deal.
世界上有許多比餐桌禮儀更重要的事。用錯餐具或是偶爾打個飽嗝之類的，我不覺得是什麼了不起的大事。

重要單字片語

- **fellow** [ˈfɛlo] *a.* 同伴的
- **rude** [rud] *a.* 無禮的，粗魯的

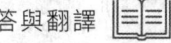

- **silverware** [ˈsɪlvɚˌwer] *n.*（刀、叉、湯匙）餐具（集合名詞，不可數）
- **burp** [bɝp] *vi.* 打飽嗝

例 It is not polite of you to burp in public.
當眾打飽嗝是不禮貌的。

- **occasionally** [əˈkeʒənlɪ] *adv.* 偶爾

❻ What do you think is the main benefit of learning a second language?
你認為學習第二語言主要的好處是什麼？

示範回答

① To me, the primary advantage of learning another language—in my case, English—is that I can communicate with people from all over the world. English is an international language, so it breaks down barriers between people of different nationalities.
對我來說，學習另一種語言 —— 以我來說是英語 —— 的最大好處是：我可以跟世界各地的人溝通。英語是國際語言，打破了不同國籍的人之間的隔閡。

② The main benefit of learning a second language is to be able to use it when you are traveling. For instance, if you learn Korean, you can use it to communicate your needs and make inquiries when you visit South Korea.
學習第二語言的最大好處就是在旅行時可以用得到。例如你學了韓文，去南韓旅遊時就可以用韓文傳達你的需求以及問問題。

重要單字片語

- **barrier** [ˈbærɪr] *n.* 障礙（物）
  break down barriers 消弭隔閡，打破藩籬
- **nationality** [ˌnæʃəˈnælətɪ] *n.* 國籍；民族
- **inquiry** [ɪnˈkwaɪrɪ] *n.* 詢問（與介詞 about 並用）
  make an inquiry about... 詢問……

❼ You notice a leak in the ceiling of your apartment. What will you do about it?
你注意到公寓的天花板有一處漏水的地方。你會怎麼做？

示範回答

① First of all, I will contact my upstairs neighbor because the leak must be coming from her apartment. If I can't get in touch with her, I will call the building manager to let him know about the urgent situation.
首先我會聯絡樓上的鄰居，因為漏水一定是源自她的公寓。如果我聯絡不到她，我會打給大樓管理員，通知這個緊急狀況。

② If there's a leak in the ceiling, I will immediately find a bucket to collect the water so that our furniture doesn't get wet. Then, I will shout for my dad. He's very handy, so he will know how to deal with the leak.
如果天花板上有漏水的話，我會馬上找水桶來接水，這樣我們的傢俱才不會弄溼。然後我會大聲喊我爸來。他修繕方面很厲害，所以他會知道怎麼處理漏水。

重要單字片語

- **leak** [lik] *vi. & n.* 漏（水、油、瓦斯等）
- **ceiling** [ˈsilɪŋ] *n.* 天花板
- **upstairs** [ˈʌpˌstɛrz] *a.* 樓上的
- **get in touch with sb** 與某人聯絡

例 Please get in touch with me as soon as possible.
請儘快跟我聯絡。

TEST 1

TEST 1

- **urgent** [ˈɝdʒənt] *a.* 緊急的；迫切的
- **furniture** [ˈfɝnɪtʃɚ] *n.* 傢俱（集合名詞，不可數）
  a piece of furniture　一件傢俱
- **handy** [ˈhændɪ] *a.* 善於修繕的，手巧的

❽ Do you order fast food often? What are the pros and cons of eating fast food?
你時常叫速食來吃嗎？吃速食的優缺點是什麼？

示範回答

① I get fast food around twice a month. The advantages of fast food are that it is readily available, relatively inexpensive, and very tasty to eat. Providing that you only consume it as an occasional treat, it is an acceptable part of a balanced diet.
我每個月大概吃兩次速食。它的優點是隨點隨到、相對便宜，味道也不錯。只要你把速食當作偶一為之的小確幸，它是可以包含在均衡飲食當中的。

② I seldom eat fast food because it is so unhealthy. In fact, I can't recall when I last ate it. It is often extremely greasy, and eating too much of it can lead to weight gain and health issues.
我很少吃速食，因為很不健康。其實我已經不記得上次吃速食是什麼時候了。速食通常相當油膩，吃太多會導致體重增加和健康問題。

重要單字片語

- **pros and cons**
  （某事物的）優點與缺點，利與弊
  例 There are pros and cons to working abroad, but I'd go for it if I were you.
  在國外工作有利有弊，但如果是我的話，我會放手一搏。

- **advantage** [ədˈvæntɪdʒ] *n.* 優點；益處
- **providing** [prəˈvaɪdɪŋ] *conj.* 如果，要是
- **acceptable** [əkˈsɛptəbl̩] *a.* 可接受的
- **recall** [rɪˈkɔl] *vt.* 回想，憶起，記得
  recall + N/V-ing　　記得……
  例 I don't recall seeing that girl before.
  我不記得以前曾見過那個女孩子。
- **greasy** [ˈgrisɪ] *a.* 油膩的
- **gain** [gen] *n.* 增加；獲得

❾ If you could visit any country in the world, where would you choose to go?
如果你可以去世上任何一個國家觀光的話，你會選擇去哪裡？

示範回答

① I would go to Indonesia. More specifically, I would visit the island of Bali. I've watched countless YouTube videos about it: the beaches look amazing, the food looks awesome, and the locals seem welcoming. Besides that, the culture is supposed to be unique and fascinating.
我會想去印尼。更精確地說，我想去峇里島。我在 YouTube 上看過太多關於那裡的影片了：沙灘看起來超讚，食物好像很好吃，當地人似乎也很好客。除此之外，島上的文化應該也是獨特又有趣的。

② I'm very interested in wildlife, so if I could go anywhere on the planet, I would choose Kenya in Africa. Going on a safari and seeing the lions, elephants, and zebras in their natural habitat would be an unforgettable experience.
我對野生動物非常感興趣，所以如果我可以去地球上任何地方的話，我會選非洲的肯亞。來趟野生動物之旅，看看獅子、大象跟斑馬在牠們的天然棲地裡，應該會是很難忘的經驗。

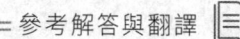

重要單字片語

- **suppose** [səˈpoz] *vt.* 想，認為；假定
  be supposed to V　應該做……
- 例 You are not supposed to wear jeans to such a formal meeting.
  你不該穿牛仔褲來參加這麼正式的會議。
- **wildlife** [ˈwaɪldˌlaɪf] *n.* 野生動植物（集合名詞，不可數）
- **safari** [səˈfɑrɪ] *n.* （觀賞野生動物的）探險旅行
- **habitat** [ˈhæbəˌtæt] *n.* （動物）棲息地
  a natural habitat　自然棲息地

❿ How big of a role do you think technology should play in education?
你認為科技在教育裡該扮演多重要的角色？

示範回答

① A huge role. Technology is an essential part of today's world, so we should be welcoming its potential to transform education. This could include using iPads for homework, artificial intelligence in teaching strategies, and virtual reality during lessons.
極為重要。科技是當今世界的基本元素，所以我們應該張開雙手擁抱它讓教育改頭換面的潛能。包括用 iPad 做家庭作業、在教學策略裡用上人工智慧，以及用虛擬實境來教課等等。

② Technology should always play a role in education, but I don't think it's the most important aspect. Nothing can beat the knowledge, insights, or advice that an inspirational teacher can provide. Also, in my opinion, using traditional books is the best way to learn.
科技應該持續在教育體系裡占有一席之地，但我不認為它是最重要的一塊。一位啟迪人心的老師所提供的知識、見解與忠告是任何事情都比不上的。而且依我之見，使用傳統書籍是最好的學習方式。

重要單字片語

- **technology** [tɛkˈnɑlədʒɪ] *n.* 科技
- **education** [ˌɛdʒəˈkeʃən] *n.* 教育
- **strategy** [ˈstrætədʒɪ] *n.* 策略，謀略
- **virtual** [ˈvɝtʃʊəl] *a.* 虛擬的；幾乎的
  virtual reality　虛擬實境
- **aspect** [ˈæspɛkt] *n.* 層面，方面
- **insight** [ˈɪnˌsaɪt] *n.* 深入理解，深刻見解
- **inspirational** [ˌɪnspəˈreʃənl] *a.* 有啟發性的；鼓舞人心的

◉ **第三部分：看圖敘述**　🔊 143

示範回答

The photo shows a man delivering a package to a woman at her door. The man, wearing a mask and gloves, is a delivery driver and is handing the item to the woman. The woman is standing at the door and accepting the package. This is a very common situation these days. Internet shopping is hugely popular, so thousands of delivery drivers deliver countless packages to people every single day. I use this kind of service on occasion. However, as I am

TEST 1

not usually at home when my items are delivered, my mom tends to sign for and accept the packages. I think that it is a fast and convenient way to receive goods, and it avoids the need to travel to a store personally.

　　這張照片顯示男子正在拿一個包裹給站在門口的女子。戴著口罩跟手套的男子是貨運司機，正把貨品交給女子。女子站在門口接下包裹。現在這種情況很常見。網路購物非常受歡迎，所以每天都有數千名貨運司機遞送多到數不清的包裹給民眾。我偶爾會利用這種服務。不過由於我時常不在家，貨品送來時通常是我媽簽名收下包裹。我覺得這種服務是快又方便的收貨方式，讓我們沒必要親自跑去店裡買東西。

重要單字片語

- **deliver** [dɪˋlɪvɚ] *vt. & vi.* 遞送，投遞
  例 We guarantee to deliver your goods tomorrow.
  我們保證明天會送貨。

- **countless** [ˋkaʊntləs] *a.* 數不盡的

GEPT 中級複試模擬測驗 第 ❷ 回　參考解答與翻譯

寫作能力測驗

◉ 第一部分：中譯英

朗達（Rhonda）在最新款的 iPhone 發售當天就跑去排隊買。她買到了當天那家分店的最後一支 iPhone 超興奮，迫不及待想回家開始連上 Wi-Fi 玩一整天的遊戲。很不巧她錯過了一班公車，而且下一班一小時後才會來！當她終於到家時，她的同事 call 她一起去打籃球。朗達勉為其難地答應去打球，但她真正想做的是玩她的新手機啊！

參考解答

Rhonda got in the long line to buy the newest iPhone model on the day it was released. She was so excited when she got the last iPhone available in the Apple Store that day, and she couldn't wait to get home, connect to Wi-Fi, and play games for the rest of the day. Unfortunately, she missed her bus and the next one didn't arrive until an hour later! When she finally got home, her colleagues called her asking her to play basketball with them. Rhonda reluctantly agreed to play, but what she really wanted was to play with her new smartphone!

重要單字片語

- **reluctantly** [rɪˋlʌktəntlɪ] *adv.* 勉為其難地，不情願地

◉ 第二部分：英文作文

有些人在閒暇的時候特別喜歡主動去認識不同的朋友，有些人則只喜歡與自己相處。請寫一篇文章
❶ 你是外向的人還是內向的人？
❷ 你喜歡與人社交嗎？為什麼？

參考解答

An extrovert is someone who enjoys being with other people, while an introvert favors being alone. I would definitely describe myself as the former. I can cope with spending time on my own, but I prefer group activities: I am comfortable with public speaking, I am a member of the school drama club, and I love team sports more than solitary leisure activities.

I enjoy socializing with other people. Not only do I frequently organize events for my friends, but I also attend parties where I don't know many people. I am happy chatting to strangers and can strike up a conversation with almost anyone. This is probably because I come from a large family, so I'm used to attending events with lots of people.

外向的人喜歡與他人相處，而內向的人偏愛獨處。我肯定會稱自己是屬於前者。我可以獨處，沒有問題，但我比較喜歡團體活動：我對著很多人說話時很自如；我是學校話劇社社員；我比較喜歡團隊運動而不是一個人的休閒活動。

我喜歡與他人社交。我不僅時常主辦朋友間的聚會，也會去參加有許多陌生人的派對。我很樂意跟陌生人閒聊，而且可以跟幾乎任何人聊得來。這可能是因為我來自大家庭，所以很習慣參加人多的活動。

重要單字片語

- **extrovert** [ˋɛkstrə͵vɝt] *n.* 外向的人 & *a.* 外向的
  introvert [ˋɪntrə͵vɝt] *n.* 內向的人 & *a.* 內向的

TEST 2

- **socialize** [ˈsoʃəˌlaɪz] *vi.* 與人交際
  socialize with sb　　與某人交際
- 例 Duke wasn't interested in socializing with other classmates.
  杜克並不想跟班上同學交際。
- **strike up a conversation with sb**
  與某人攀談
- 例 You can strike up a conversation with people by talking about the weather.
  你若想跟人開啟話頭，可以先談天氣。

口說能力測驗

第一部分：朗讀短文　🔊 144

Rita is organizing a surprise birthday party for her best friend Jenny. She has found a suitable location and bought some balloons which will be used to decorate the place. She has pre-ordered the food from a local restaurant that Jenny frequently goes to. She has also hired a DJ and informed him of Jenny's favorite tunes. Now all she needs to do is send out invitations to their classmates and pray that no one spills the beans about the celebration.

　　瑞塔正在為她最好的朋友珍妮籌劃驚喜生日派對。她已經找到適合的場地，又買了裝飾場地用的氣球。她已經從珍妮常去的某家當地餐廳預訂好餐點。她也雇用了一個 DJ，而且跟他叮囑了珍妮最愛的歌曲。現在她該做的只剩下寄邀請函給她們班上的同學，然後祈禱他們不會把慶祝會的消息洩漏出去。

重要單字片語

- **organize** [ˈɔrgəˌnaɪz] *vt.* 籌辦，組織
- **suitable** [ˈsutəbḷ] *a.* 適當的
- **location** [loˈkeʃən] *n.* 地點

- **decorate** [ˈdɛkəˌret] *vt.* 裝飾
  decorate A with B　　用 B 布置 A
- 例 Mom decorated the new house with original artwork from India.
  媽媽用印度的原創工藝品裝飾新房子。
- **frequently** [ˈfrikwəntlɪ] *adv.* 經常
- 例 You can frequently see celebrities in this restaurant.
  你經常會在這家餐廳看到名人。
- **tune** [tjun] *n.* 曲調，旋律
- **invitation** [ˌɪnvəˈteʃən] *n.* 請帖，邀請卡；邀請
- **spill the beans**　　洩漏祕密，走漏風聲
- 例 I'm going to tell you a secret, but please don't spill the beans to anyone else.
  我要告訴你一個祕密，但請千萬不要洩漏出去。

The first cell phone was invented around five decades ago, but it was not until the 1990s that these devices became small and portable enough to be used extensively. At this time, people could send text messages, play elementary games, and use functions like calendars and reminders on their phones. It was not until 2007 that the smartphone, as many people would call it, came into being. Combining a touchscreen with internet access and downloadable apps, the smartphone transformed the communications and electronics industries.

　　第一支手機大概在五十年前就已經發明了，但是直到 1990 年代，手機才變得夠小而且方便攜帶，進而被廣泛使用。當時大家可以在手機上傳簡訊、玩簡單的遊戲以及使用日曆與提醒訊息等功能。直到 2007 年，許多人口中的智慧型手機才問世。結合觸控螢幕、上網功能與可下載應用程式的智慧手機改變了通訊與電子產業。

重要單字片語

- **device** [dɪˈvaɪs] *n.* 裝置；設計
- **portable** [ˈpɔrtəb!] *a.* 可攜帶的
- **extensively** [ɪkˈstɛnsɪvlɪ] *adv.* 廣泛地；廣大地
- **elementary** [ˌɛləˈmɛntərɪ] *a.* 基本的；初級的，基礎的
- **access** [ˈæksɛs] *n.*（對人、地、物的）接近或使用的權利或門徑
- **transform** [trænsˈfɔrm] *vt.* 改變，變化
例 The landowner transformed the old house into a hotel.
地主將這棟老房子改建成旅館。

◉ 第二部分：回答問題 🔊 145

❶ Do you like Halloween? Do you enjoy wearing costumes on that night?
你喜歡萬聖節嗎？你喜歡在那天晚上穿奇裝異服嗎？

示範回答

① I love Halloween. I enjoy being creative and making my own costumes, and my friends and I always attend a big Halloween party.
我喜歡萬聖節。我喜歡發揮創意，自己製作服裝，而且我跟朋友都會參加大型萬聖節派對。

② To be honest, I think Halloween is a bit silly. Wearing costumes is fine for little kids, but it's not suitable for teenagers and adults.
老實說，我覺得萬聖節有點傻氣。穿奇裝異服對小孩來說還可以，但青少年跟大人就不必了。

重要單字片語

- **costume** [ˈkɑst(j)um] *n.* 服裝（尤指戲服或民族服裝）；（特殊節日的）奇裝異服
- **creative** [krɪˈetɪv] *a.* 有創造力的
- **attend** [əˈtɛnd] *vt. & vi.* 參加，出席
例 A lot of people attended the hero's funeral.
大批民眾前往參加那位英雄的葬禮。
- **silly** [ˈsɪlɪ] *a.* 愚蠢的

❷ Have you ever experienced a power outage? How did you react?
你有碰過停電嗎？你當時作何反應？

示範回答

① Yes. The power went out in my apartment once during a typhoon. It was a little scary, but luckily we had bought some candles.
有。有次颱風來，我的公寓曾一度停電。有點可怕，還好我們事先有買好蠟燭。

② No, I've never had that experience. If I did, I would try to remain calm and use the light on my smartphone.
我從沒碰過停電。如果碰上了，我會試著保持冷靜，然後用智慧手機上的手電筒。

重要單字片語

- **outage** [ˈaʊtɪdʒ] *n.*（水、電等的）中斷供應
  a power outage　　停電
- **react** [rɪˈækt] *vi.* 反應（與介詞 to 並用）
  react to sth　　對某事物有反應
例 Carl reacted to the news by shaking his head in silence.
卡爾對這消息的反應是搖搖頭，什麼話也沒說。
- **remain** [rɪˈmen] *vi.* 仍是（之後接名詞或形容詞作補語）
  remain healthy　　保持健康
- **calm** [kɑm] *a.* 冷靜的

❸ Have you ever lost your phone? Tell me what happened.
你曾經把手機弄丟過嗎？怎麼回事？

TEST 2

示範回答

① My phone is by far my most valued possession, so I'm very careful with it. Consequently, I've never lost it.
我的手機是我最最最貴重的財產，所以我非常小心。因為如此，我從來沒弄丟過手機。

② I lost my phone once. I don't know for sure, but I think I left it on a bus. I had no option but to purchase a new one.
我弄丟過一次。我不敢確定，但應該是把手機忘在公車上了。沒辦法，我只好買新手機。

重要單字片語

- **possession** [pəˈzɛʃən] *n.* 所有物
- **consequently** [ˈkɑnsəˌkwɛntlɪ] *adv.* 因此，所以
- **purchase** [ˈpɝtʃəs] *vt. & n.* 購買
  例 Rather than purchase new shoes, Randy paid someone to sole his old pair.
  蘭迪沒有買新鞋，而是花錢找人幫他的舊鞋換雙鞋底。

❹ The person next to you in the library is being noisy. What will you do?
在圖書館裡，你旁邊的人很吵。你會怎麼做？

示範回答

① If the person is being annoying—for example, talking loudly on the phone—I will simply find another seat in the library.
如果那個人很惹人嫌，例如大聲講電話之類的，我會直接去找圖書館裡的其他座位。

② I will turn to the person and politely ask him or her to stop making noise. I'll try to explain that libraries are supposed to be quiet places for study.
我會轉向那個人，禮貌地要求他 / 她停止製造噪音。我會解釋說圖書館應該是讓人安靜讀書的地方。

重要單字片語

- **library** [ˈlaɪˌbrɛrɪ] *n.* 圖書館
- **annoying** [əˈnɔɪɪŋ] *a.* 討厭的，煩人的
- **politely** [pəˈlaɪtlɪ] *adv.* 有禮貌地
- **quiet** [ˈkwaɪət] *a.* 安靜的

❺ Should homework be banned? Please explain your answer.
我們應該禁絕家庭作業嗎？請說明你的答案。

示範回答

① Homework plays a vital role in learning. There isn't enough time in class for students to practice everything, so I won't justify banning it.
家庭作業是學習上重要的一環。在課堂上是沒有足夠時間讓學生做大量練習的，所以我不會把不做作業合理化。

② The amount of homework should definitely be reduced significantly, but homework should not be banned completely. We should have more time to relax at home, but doing nothing is not acceptable, either.
家庭作業的量絕對該大幅減少，但家庭作業不該被完全禁絕。我們在家裡需要更多休息時間，但什麼都不做也是不行的。

重要單字片語

- **ban** [bæn] *vt.* 下令禁止（三態為：ban, banned [bænd], banned）
  例 Most countries have banned shark finning.
  大多數國家都已禁止獵鯊取翅的行為。

- **justify** [ˋdʒʌstəˌfaɪ] *vt.* 證明……是合理的，使合理化（三態為：justify, justified [ˋdʒʌstəfaɪd], justified）

例 Sam couldn't justify making everyone wait for him.
對於讓大家等他一人，山姆無法自圓其說。

- **significantly** [sɪgˋnɪfəkəntlɪ] *adv.* 大大地，可觀地

- **relax** [rɪˋlæks] *vi.* 放鬆，休息

例 Listening to music can help me relax.
聽音樂可以幫助我放鬆。

---

❻ What characteristics make a really good friend? Do you have a friend like that?
摯友的人格特質為何？你有這樣的朋友嗎？

示範回答

① A really good friend should be loyal and trustworthy. You should be able to rely on him or her to be honest with you, keep your secrets, and always be there during the good times and the bad times. My best friend Chris is exactly like that.
一個真正的好朋友應該要不離不棄且值得信任。你可以信賴他／她會對你誠實、幫你保守祕密，並且陪你走過人生的起起伏伏。我最好的朋友克里斯就是這樣的人。

② My best friend Tina is a perfect example of a really good friend. She always listens to me without judging me; she respects my decisions even when she doesn't agree with them; and she has an amazing sense of humor!
我最好的朋友蒂娜就是摯友的完美範例。她總是聆聽而不批判；即使不認同但仍會尊重我的決定；而且她的幽默感太讚了！

重要單字片語

- **characteristic** [ˌkærəktəˋrɪstɪk] *n.* 特徵
- **loyal** [ˋlɔɪəl] *a.* 忠誠的
- **trustworthy** [ˋtrʌstˌwɝðɪ] *a.* 值得信賴的
- **rely** [rɪˋlaɪ] *vi.* 依賴；信賴（三態為：rely, relied [rɪˋlaɪd], relied）
  rely on / upon... 依賴……；信賴……

例 I trust Steve very much. I know he is a man I can always rely on.
我很信任史提夫。我知道他是一個可信賴的人。

- **judge** [dʒʌdʒ] *vt.* 審判；裁判；判斷
- **decision** [dɪˋsɪʒən] *n.* 決定

---

❼ Name a sport that is popular in your country. Do you like to play it or watch it?
說說在你的國家裡受歡迎的某種運動。你想玩它嗎？還是只想當觀眾？

示範回答

① Basketball is a very popular sport in my country. Many of my peers play it, either for fun or as part of a team that competes. However, it is not a sport that I like to play or even watch.
籃球在我的國家很受歡迎。許多我的同輩都會打籃球，或為消遣，或為組隊比賽。不過我對此運動是既不想玩也不會看。

② One of the most popular sports in Taiwan is baseball. I do play it occasionally, but I am much more interested in watching it. I follow a local team, and I regularly watch their games at various stadiums.
棒球是臺灣人氣最高的運動之一。我偶爾會打一打，但對看更有興趣。我有關注一支本地球隊，常去不同的運動場看他們比賽。

TEST 2

TEST 2

重要單字片語

- **name** [nem] *vt.* 說出……的名稱；選出；命名
- **popular** [ˈpɑpjələ] *a.* 受歡迎的
- **peer** [pɪr] *n.* 同輩，同儕
- **regularly** [ˈrɛgjələlɪ] *adv.* 固定地
- **stadium** [ˈstedɪəm] *n.* 體育場

❽ Is there a famous person that you admire? Tell me about him or her.
你有特別欽佩某個名人嗎？跟我聊聊他 / 她。

示範回答

① A famous person I admire is Elon Musk. I think his desire to make space travel more affordable is very inspirational. He's also involved in Tesla, which has revolutionized electric vehicles, and X, which is committed to free speech.
我欣賞的名人之一是伊隆・馬斯克。我覺得他想讓太空旅遊變得更便宜的願望是很了不起的。他也有經營帶動電動汽車革命的特斯拉，以及全力推動言論自由的 X。

② I admire Steve Jobs for the role he played in founding Apple and developing and launching the iPhone, even though he has passed away. In my opinion, his hard work and genius have changed our lives for the better.
我欣賞史提夫・賈伯斯在創立蘋果公司以及研發並推出 iPhone 時所扮演的角色，儘管他已經過世了。依我的淺見，他的努力與天賦讓我們的生活更多采多姿了。

重要單字片語

- **admire** [əd'maɪr] *vt.* 欣賞，欽佩
  admire sb for sth　因某事物而欣賞某人

例 I admire Justin for his proficiency in English.
我很欽佩賈斯汀的英文造詣。

- **desire** [dɪˈzaɪr] *n.* 渴望，慾望
- **revolutionize** [ˌrɛvəˈluʃəˌnaɪz] *vt.*（徹底）改革

例 The techniques developed at this lab have revolutionized heart surgery.
這個實驗室所研發出來的技術徹底改變了心臟手術。

- **found** [faʊnd] *vt.* 建立，創辦（三態為：found, founded [ˈfaʊndɪd], founded）

例 Our school was founded 85 years ago.
本校於八十五年前創立。

- **pass away**　去世，過世
- **genius** [ˈdʒinjəs] *n.* 天賦，天分

❾ Do you think children should have privacy? Why or why not?
你覺得兒童應該有隱私嗎？試述其理由。

示範回答

① Older kids and teenagers definitely deserve privacy. They need their own space so that they can grow emotionally and become independent without feeling watched or judged. Parents should demonstrate that they trust their children and value their personal boundaries.
年紀稍大的兒童與青少年確實應該享有隱私。他們需要自己的空間，才能在沒有感覺受到監視或評斷的情況下，培養成熟的情緒並學會獨立。父母應該展現信任孩子的度量，並尊重他們的隱私界線。

② By their very nature, children need guidance, supervision, and protection. Kids are not always aware of potential

dangers—from strangers or people online, for instance—so their privacy should be limited. Being safe is ultimately more important than having privacy.
兒童天生就是需要人指引、監督跟保護的。小孩子沒法隨時注意到潛在的危險，例如危險的陌生人或網路上的網民。所以他們的隱私應該受到限制。安全比起隱私來得重要太多了。

重要單字片語

- privacy [ˈpraɪvəsɪ] *n.* 隱私（不可數）
- deserve [dɪˈzɝv] *vt.* 應得

例 Such a hardworking man really deserves a raise.
這麼努力工作的人值得加薪。

- value [ˈvæljʊ] *vt.* 珍惜

例 Sam will always value your friendship.
山姆會永遠珍惜你的友誼。

- boundary [ˈbaʊnd(ə)rɪ] *n.* 邊界，分界線；界限
- guidance [ˈɡaɪdəns] *n.* 指導（不可數）
- supervision [ˌsupɚˈvɪʒən] *n.* 監督，管理（不可數）

⑩ How important do you think it is to have a fixed daily routine?
你覺得固定的每日活動行程有多重要？

示範回答

① I think it is very important to have a fixed routine every day. It helps to give our lives much-needed structure. If we don't have fixed routines, like those at school and work, life will definitely be chaos.
我覺得很重要。它可以把我們的生活裝進必須該有的一個架構裡。如果我們沒有如學校與職場那樣的固定行程，人生一定就會如同一團亂麻。

② Of course, there has got to be some routine in our lives. However, if we just follow the same routine every day, our life will become very boring. We need to break routines every now and then and challenge ourselves by trying new things and going to new places.
我們的生活裡當然得有例行公事。不過要是我們每天都只遵循例行公事，生活就會變得很乏味。我們得三不五時去打破一下規律，去嘗試新的事物、去沒去過的地方以挑戰自我。

重要單字片語

- fixed [fɪkst] *a.* 固定的
- routine [ruˈtin] *n.* 慣例，例行公事 & *a.* 例行公事的
  a daily routine 每天的例行公事
- structure [ˈstrʌktʃɚ] *n.* 結構
- chaos [ˈkeɑs] *n.* 混亂（不可數）
  be in chaos 混亂

◉ 第三部分：看圖敘述　🔊 146

示範回答

This is a photograph taken in a clothing store. Two women are standing and one man is sitting. There are multiple items of clothing hung in the background. One of the women is pointing to a blouse she is holding. Her body language implies she is seeking the man's opinion. The smile on her face indicates she is enjoying the experience in the store. I enjoy shopping for clothes, too. Purchasing a new sweater or pair of jeans makes me feel happy and content. Of course, I can't always afford to buy new clothes, but even simply trying them on is a very satisfying activity. I especially enjoy going with my friends so that we can comment on each other's choices and encourage each other to try different styles.

　　這張照片是在服裝店裡拍的，有兩個女子站著，一個男子坐著。在他們身後有許多衣服掛著。女子之一指著手裡拿的一件上衣。她的肢體語言顯示她正在尋求男子的意見。她臉上的笑容顯示她很享受在店內的體驗。我也喜歡買衣服。買新毛衣或牛仔褲讓我感到幸福又滿足。當然，我沒辦法總是有錢買新衣服，但即便只是試穿，也是很滿足的事情。我特別喜歡跟朋友一起去，這樣就可以給彼此選的衣物品頭論足，並鼓勵彼此嘗試不同的款式。

重要單字片語

- **multiple** [ˈmʌltəpl] *a.* 眾多的；多重的
- **imply** [ɪmˈplaɪ] *vt.* 暗示（三態為：imply, implied [ɪmˈplaɪd], implied）
  例 Mike is implying that he doesn't want to continue with this class anymore.
  麥克暗示自己不想再繼續上這門課。
- **indicate** [ˈɪndəˌket] *vt.* 顯示，表明
- **afford** [əˈfɔrd] *vt.* 負擔得起
  can / cannot afford N / to V
  有 / 無能力負擔得起 / 從事……
  例 I cannot afford to buy a brand-new car.
  我買不起全新的汽車。

- **comment** [ˈkɑmɛnt] *vi.* 評論
  comment on... 評論……
  例 I refuse to comment on what Gary has done.
  我拒絕就蓋瑞的所作所為發表任何評論。

GEPT 中級複試模擬測驗 第 ❸ 回 參考解答與翻譯

寫作能力測驗

◉ 第一部分：中譯英

彼得（Peter）退休時很擔心人生會失去目標。因此他決定要參與慈善志工服務。雖然捐錢又快又簡單，但他想要奉獻他的時間。他選擇了一間幫助窮苦三餐不繼民眾的地方慈善機構。他首先主辦了一場烘焙義賣來募款。後來他協助將超市捐贈的食物打包裝盒。彼得感到很滿足，因為他可以在社區裡幫助那些需要幫助的人。

參考解答

When Peter retired, he was concerned about lacking a purpose in life, so he decided to volunteer for charity. Rather than donating money, which was quick and easy, he wanted to give his time. He chose a local charity that helped the poor and hungry. First, he organized a bake sale to raise money. Then, he helped pack boxes of food that had been donated by supermarkets. Peter felt content that he was able to assist those in need in his community.

重要單字片語

- **purpose** [ˋpɝpəs] *n.* 目的
- **volunteer** [ˌvɑlənˋtɪr] *vi.* 自告奮勇 & *n.* 自願者，義工
- **charity** [ˋtʃærətɪ] *n.* 慈善（不可數）；慈善機構（可數）
- **donate** [ˋdonet / doˋnet] *vt.* & *vi.* 捐獻（金錢、物資等）
- **content** [kənˋtɛnt] *a.* 滿足的

◉ 第二部分：英文作文

每到旅遊旺季的期間，各地都充滿著觀光客，大家都想趁機放鬆一下，並且為自己留下美好的回憶。請寫一篇文章

❶ 你旅行時喜歡買紀念品嗎？為什麼？
❷ 如果有，哪一個紀念品對你來說最特別？如果沒有，你會以什麼方式回憶每次的旅行？

參考解答

I love traveling, from day trips in Taiwan to two-week-long vacations abroad. Wherever I go, I like to buy a souvenir. It's usually inexpensive small things—typically a fridge magnet or a miniature model of a building. Nevertheless, it helps me remember the trip and the fun time I had with my friends or family.

The souvenir that I consider the most special is a snow globe of Mount Fuji in Japan. It is a relatively simple souvenir, but I feel a deep emotional connection to it. That's because my grandma bought it for me, and that trip to Japan was the only vacation I went on with my grandparents.

我愛旅遊，從臺灣的一日遊到兩週的國外假期都一樣喜歡。不論去哪裡，我都喜歡買紀念品，通常是不貴的小東西，主要如冰箱磁鐵或建築物的小模型等等。但是紀念品可以幫我記住那趟旅遊以及我與親朋好友共度的歡樂時光。

我認為最特別的紀念品是日本富士山的雪花玻璃球。它算蠻普通的紀念品，但我對它有很深的情感連結。因為那是奶奶買給我的，而那次日本行是我跟爺爺奶奶僅有的一次共同出遊。

重要單字片語

- **abroad** [əˋbrɔd] *adv.* 在國外；到國外
- **souvenir** [ˋsuvəˌnɪr] *n.* 紀念品；紀念物
- **magnet** [ˋmægnɪt] *n.* 磁鐵
  a fridge magnet 冰箱磁鐵
- **relatively** [ˋrɛlətɪvlɪ] *adv.* 相對地

TEST 3

17

TEST 3

口說能力測驗

第一部分：朗讀短文 🔊 147

  Earlier this year, I went to Germany with my older brother. He intends to study there someday and wanted to learn more about the place. He really enjoyed traveling around the country, and I did too. However, after a few days, I began to miss Taiwanese food, especially my mom's cooking. I got tired of the freezing weather and being unable to speak the language. I realized that I had a serious case of homesickness. I couldn't wait to go back to Taiwan—a warm place with the best food in the world.

  今年稍早，我跟我哥一起去德國玩。他想將來去那裡讀書，想多了解一下那個國家。他真的很享受德國之行，我也是。不過幾天後我就開始想念臺灣的食物，尤其是我媽煮的菜。我厭倦了冷颼颼的天氣以及不會說德語的不便。我知道我得了嚴重的思鄉病。我等不及想回臺灣——一個又溫暖又有世界頂級美食的地方。

重要單字片語

- **intend** [ɪnˋtɛnd] *vt.* 意欲，想要
  intend to V 想要做……
  例 What do you intend to do with your life after you graduate?
  畢業後你想如何安排生活？

- **realize** [ˋrɪəˌlaɪz] *vt.* 意識到

  Museums play an essential role in preserving history. They collect objects from the past and ensure these are kept safe for future generations. They store everything from historical documents to paintings to ancient tools, all of which give visitors a glimpse into different cultures, societies, and time periods. Museums serve as a vital educational resource, helping to make sure that we learn the lessons of the past and reducing our chances of repeating our ancestors' mistakes.

  博物館在保存歷史方面扮演著關鍵角色。博物館蒐集過去的文物，確保它們得到妥善的保存以傳承給未來的世代。博物館的收藏包羅萬象，從歷史文獻到繪畫再到古老工具，每件物品都讓參觀者得以窺探不同的文化、社會和歷史時期。博物館是重要的教育資源，有助於我們從歷史當中汲取教訓，以減少重蹈祖先錯誤的機會。

重要單字片語

- **preserve** [prɪˋzɝv] *vt.* 保存
  例 The villagers salted and dried the fish to preserve it.
  村民將魚鹽醃並風乾以利保存。

- **ensure** [ɪnˋʃʊr] *vt.* 確保
  例 Hard work ensures success.
  努力定會成功。

- **store** [stor] *vt.* 儲存
  例 This flash drive stores a lot of information.
  這個隨身碟儲存了許多資料。

- **historical** [hɪsˋtɔrɪkḷ] *a.* 與歷史有關的

- **glimpse** [glɪmps] *n. & vt.* 瞥見

- **educational** [ˌɛdʒəˋkeʃənḷ] *a.* 教育的；教育性的

- **reduce** [rɪˋd(j)us] *vt.* 減少
  例 The boss summarized the meeting by saying that we needed to reduce costs.
  老闆總結會議時表明我們需要減少支出。

- **ancestor** [ˋænsɛstɚ] *n.* 祖先

第二部分：回答問題 🔊 148

❶ What do you do to prevent yourself from catching a cold or the flu?
你如何預防得感冒或流感？

示範回答

① To stop myself from getting sick, I wear a face mask when I go to crowded indoor places. That way, I have some level of protection against other people's germs.
為了防止自己染病，我去人多的室內地點時會戴口罩。這麼一來，我就對他人的病菌有了某種程度的保護。

② I wash my hands frequently and thoroughly with soap and water, and then I dry them properly. That's the most effective way to prevent illness.
我常用肥皂水仔細地洗手，然後好好把手擦乾。這是預防疾病最有效的方法。

重要單字片語

- **prevent** [prɪˋvɛnt] *vt.* 預防，避免；阻止
  prevent A from B　　避免 A 受 B 所害
- 例 Mr. Davis remained neutral on the issue to prevent himself from getting into trouble.
  戴維斯先生在該議題上保持中立，以免惹上麻煩。
- **flu** [flu] *n.* 流行性感冒（= influenza [ˌɪnfluˋɛnzə]）（不可數）
  have / get / catch the flu　　得到流感
- **indoor** [ˋɪnˌdor] *a.* 室內的
- **germ** [dʒɝm] *n.* 細菌，病菌
- **thoroughly** [ˋθɝolɪ] *adv.* 徹底地，完全地
- **properly** [ˋprɑpɚlɪ] *adv.* 適當地；正確地
- **effective** [ɪˋfɛktɪv] *a.* 有效的

❷ Have you ever volunteered for a charity? Why or why not?
你曾經在慈善機構當過志工嗎？請解釋理由。

示範回答

① No, I've never volunteered for a charity. I think it's an admirable thing to do, but I've never had enough time due to schoolwork and household chores.
我沒有在慈善機構當過志工。我覺得做志工是值得欽佩的，但由於忙於課業與家務，我一直沒有足夠的時間去參與。

② Yes, I volunteer at an animal shelter twice a month because I love animals. I help walk the dogs and clean the cages.
有，因為我喜歡動物，所以有去一家動物收容所當志工，每個月兩次。我幫忙遛狗以及清理籠子。

重要單字片語

- **volunteer** [ˌvɑlənˋtɪr] *vi.* 自告奮勇
- 例 The taxi driver volunteered to help.
  這位計程車司機自告奮勇要幫忙。
- **charity** [ˋtʃærətɪ] *n.* 慈善機構（可數）；慈善（不可數）
- **admirable** [ˋædmərəb!] *a.* 值得讚美的，令人欽佩的
- **chore** [tʃor] *n.* 雜務
  household chores　　家事
- **cage** [kedʒ] *n.* 籠子

❸ Do you follow a religion? Do you find this helpful in your daily life?
你信教嗎？你覺得這對你的生活有幫助嗎？

示範回答

① Yes, I am a Buddhist. If I am feeling confused about something, I go to a temple and seek guidance, which I find very helpful.
我是佛教徒。如果我對某事感到困惑，會去寺廟尋求指引，我覺得很有幫助。

TEST 3

② No, I am not a religious person. If I needed help in my daily life, I would talk to a friend or family member rather than a god.
我沒有宗教信仰。如果我在生活中需要幫助，會去找朋友或家人聊聊，不會去找神明。

重要單字片語

- religion [rɪˋlɪdʒən] n. 宗教（信仰）
  religious [rɪˋlɪdʒəs] a. 虔誠的；宗教的
- Buddhist [ˋbʊdɪst] n. 佛教徒 & a. 佛教的
- seek [sik] vt. 尋找（三態為：seek, sought [sɔt] , sought）

例 The government is seeking new ways to fight crime.
政府正在尋找新的方法來打擊犯罪。

❹ What is your favorite way to exercise? Tell me why.
你最喜歡的運動方式是什麼？請解釋理由。

示範回答

① My favorite form of exercise is slow jogging. It sounds easy, but you have to take 180 or 190 steps per minute, so it gets you very sweaty!
我最喜歡的運動就是超慢跑。它聽起來簡單，但是每分鐘要跑一百八十或一百九十步，所以會讓你滿身大汗！

② I like to do sit-ups, push-ups, and planks in my room. They are good for my body, and I don't need to spend money on a gym membership to do them.
我喜歡在房間裡做仰臥起坐、扶地挺身以及棒式。這些運動對身體很好，而我不用花錢買健身房會員就能做。

重要單字片語

- sweaty [ˋswɛtɪ] a. 多汗的
- membership [ˋmɛmbɚˌʃɪp] n. 會員身分
  a membership fee　　會費

❺ When you go outside, how do you protect yourself from the sun?
你去戶外時如何防曬？

示範回答

① I always wear suntan lotion when I go outside on sunny days. I think it's the best way to protect myself from the sun's harmful rays.
我在豔陽天外出時都會擦防曬乳。我覺得這是保護自己不被太陽有害光線曬傷的最有效方法。

② I wear a cap and a long-sleeved T-shirt when it's really hot, but I'm also aware that we need some vitamin D from the sun to stay healthy.
天氣非常熱時我會戴帽子跟穿長袖 T 恤，但我也清楚：若要保持健康，是需要曬點太陽來製造維他命 D 的。

重要單字片語

- suntan [ˋsʌntæn] n. 曬成的古銅色皮膚
  suntan lotion　　防曬乳液
- harmful [ˋhɑrmfəl] a. 有害的
- ray [re] n. 光線

❻ Name an unusual hobby that you want to try. Why would you like to try it?
舉一個你想嘗試的奇特嗜好。請解釋理由。

示範回答

① I'd like to try magnet fishing. I watched a video about it once, and it involves using magnets to search for metal objects in bodies of water. It would be interesting to see what's down there, and it might also help to keep our rivers and oceans clean.
我會想試試磁鐵垂釣。我看過相關的影片，它是用磁鐵在水域裡尋找金屬物品的活動。看看

從水裡能釣起來什麼東西是很有意思的，而且還可以幫助潔淨河川與海洋。

② I think it would be cool to try beekeeping. Caring for bees and collecting their honey sounds like a fun way to learn about nature and help to support bee populations. After all, bees play an essential role in nature.

我覺得試試養蜂應該是蠻酷的。養蜂採蜜感覺是認識大自然的有趣方式，而且還能協助保持蜜蜂的數量。畢竟蜜蜂在大自然裡扮演著相當重要的角色。

重要單字片語

- **hobby** [ˈhɑbɪ] *n.* 嗜好
- **magnet** [ˈmæɡnɪt] *n.* 磁鐵
- **metal** [ˈmɛtl̩] *n.* 金屬
- **body of water** 水域
- **population** [ˌpɑpjəˈleʃən] *n.* 動物總數；人口，全體人民

❼ Are video games good or bad for children?
電玩對兒童是好是壞？

示範回答

① I think video games have a largely positive impact on kids. They help children develop their hand-eye coordination and problem-solving skills. Plus, they are very entertaining, so they provide young people with an opportunity to unwind.

我覺得大體上電玩對兒童的影響是正面的。它可以幫他們培養手眼協調性以及解決難題的能力。況且打電玩的娛樂性很足，提供孩子們休閒的機會。

② Although some video games can be educational, I think most of them have a negative impact on children. Kids can become addicted to them, which causes their schoolwork to suffer. Also, sitting in front of a screen for too long is bad for kids' health.

雖然有些電玩是教育性質，但我覺得大部分是對兒童有負面影響的。兒童會沉迷於電動，導致成績退步。此外，長時間坐在螢幕前對兒童的健康有害。

重要單字片語

- **coordination** [koˌɔrdəˈneʃən] *n.* 協調（不可數）
- **entertaining** [ˌɛntɚˈtenɪŋ] *a.* 有娛樂性，令人愉快的
- **unwind** [ʌnˈwaɪnd] *vt. & vi.* （使）放鬆（三態為：unwind, unwound [ʌnˈwaʊnd], unwound）
- 例 Ed took a short vacation to Hawaii to unwind from his stressful job.
  為了紓解工作壓力，艾德去夏威夷小小地度了個假。
- **educational** [ˌɛdʒəˈkeʃənl̩] *a.* 教育性的；教育的
- **addict** [əˈdɪkt] *vt.* 使上癮（與介詞 to 並用）
  be / become addicted to + N/V-ing
  對……上癮
- 例 My little brother is addicted to video games.
  我的小弟沉迷電玩。

❽ What was your most unforgettable vacation?
你最難忘的假期是什麼？

示範回答

① Without a doubt, my most unforgettable vacation was the trip to India. The sights and sounds were incredible, especially when I visited the Taj Mahal. It's a

21

TEST 3

masterpiece of design and architecture. The streets around it were busy and noisy, but it was so peaceful in the gardens.

毫無疑問，我最難忘的假期是印度之旅。在那裡的所見所聞真是奇妙，尤其是參觀泰姬瑪哈陵。它是設計與建築的經典之作。其周圍的街道很繁忙吵雜，但在花園裡頭卻出奇地寧靜。

② My most memorable trip was to the US. We toured around several states and saw several iconic places, such as Hollywood and the Statue of Liberty. The food was great, too—the portions are so huge!

我最難忘的旅遊是去美國。我們去了好幾個州，看了一些代表性的景點，像是好萊塢跟自由女神像等等。美國的食物也很棒，分量真的超大！

重要單字片語

- **unforgettable** [ˌʌnfɚˈɡɛtəbḷ] *a.* 難忘的
- **doubt** [daʊt] *n.* 疑問
  without (a) doubt　毫無疑問
- **masterpiece** [ˈmæstɚˌpis] *n.* 傑作
- **architecture** [ˈɑrkəˌtɛktʃɚ] *n.* 建築（風格）
- **iconic** [aɪˈkɑnɪk] *a.* 具代表性的
- **portion** [ˈpɔrʃən] *n.* 一客食物的量；一部分

❾ Would you rather read a book or watch a movie? Tell me why.

你比較喜歡看書還是看電影？請解釋理由。

示範回答

① I would much rather watch a movie than read a book. I do so much studying and reading for school that I don't want to read in my free time. Films only last for a couple of hours, so watching one is more efficient.

我看電影的意願遠大於看書。我為了課業已經看太多書了，不想在閒暇時間還要看書。電影的片長只有兩小時，所以看電影比較省時。

② Between a book and a movie, I would almost always choose the book. Books are much richer in detail, and you can really explore the world and the characters that the author has created.

在書與電影之間，我絕大多數時間都會選擇看書。書籍裡的細節更加豐富，讓人可以深入探索書裡的世界以及作者創作的角色。

重要單字片語

- **last** [læst] *vi.* 持續
  例 The meeting lasted for more than two hours.
  這場會議進行了兩個多小時。
- **efficient** [ɪˈfɪʃənt] *a.* 有效率的
- **detail** [ˈditel] *n.* 細節
  in detail　詳細地
  例 I haven't had time to review the plan in detail yet.
  我還沒有時間詳細審閱這計畫。
- **character** [ˈkærəktɚ] *n.* （書、劇中的）角色
- **author** [ˈɔθɚ] *n.* 作者

❿ Are you or do you want to be a vegetarian? Why or why not?

你有吃素嗎？還是你有想要吃素？請解釋理由。

示範回答

① No, I am not a vegetarian, and I don't want to be one either. I enjoy eating meat and seafood too much to give them up. Besides, these are good sources of protein, and we need that to stay healthy.

我沒有吃素，而且也不想。我太愛吃肉跟海鮮了，很難放棄耶。況且肉類跟海鮮是優質的蛋白質來源，我們需要它來保持健康。

② I am a vegetarian, and I have been one for around five years. I chose to follow a vegetarian diet not only for health reasons but also because it's better for the environment. Plant-based foods require less water and energy to grow.

我吃素已經有五年左右了。我選擇吃素食不僅是為了健康，也因為這樣比較環保。種植蔬菜類食物用掉的水跟資源比較少。

重要單字片語

- **vegetarian** [ˌvɛdʒəˈtɛrɪən] *n.* 素食者
- **give up...** 放棄……
- 例 No matter what happens, never give up hope.
  不管發生什麼事，千萬不要放棄希望。
- **source** [sɔrs] *n.* 來源
- **protein** [ˈprotiɪn] *n.* 蛋白質
- **diet** [ˈdaɪət] *n.* 日常飲食；節食

🔊 第三部分：看圖敘述 149

示範回答

The image shows two women in a restaurant enjoying a meal. The women are obviously good friends as they appear to be laughing and joking with one another. The restaurant is very clean and quite casual, with a wooden table and partially tiled wall. The meal on the table consists of two bowls of soup or noodles and two plates of side dishes, such as tofu. I often share a light meal with friends. In fact, there is nothing that gives me more pleasure than trying out new restaurants and sampling simple but tasty food. I am happy doing it alone, but it's much more fun with friends or classmates who share my passion.

這照片顯示兩個女子正在餐廳吃飯。她們顯然是好友，因為她們看起來很快樂且互相有說有笑。餐廳很乾淨而且是家常風格，桌子是木頭的，牆面一部分貼有磁磚。桌上的食物包括兩碗湯或是麵之類的，另加兩盤小菜，裡面有豆腐。我常跟朋友去吃輕食。事實上，嘗試新餐館、品嚐簡單卻美味的食物是我的最愛。我也很喜歡一個人去，但若能跟同好的朋友或同學一起去更好玩。

重要單字片語

- **obviously** [ˈɑbvɪəslɪ] *adv.* 明顯地
- **partially** [ˈpɑrʃəlɪ] *adv.* 部分地
- **tiled** [taɪld] *a.* 貼著磁磚的
  a tiled wall 貼著磁磚的牆
- **consist** [kənˈsɪst] *vi.* 由……組成
  consist of... 由……組成
- 例 This new product consists of bath salts and other minerals.
  這個新產品包含浴鹽及其他的礦物質。

GEPT 中級複試模擬測驗 第 ❹ 回　參考解答與翻譯

寫作能力測驗

◉ 第一部分：中譯英

我週末時去了一個農民市集，是個在地農民把農產品直接銷售給大眾的地方。那裡有非常多攤販兜售各式各樣的食物，看起來都很好吃的樣子，香味撲鼻而來。我試吃了幾樣我最喜歡的東西：有起司、有香腸，也喝了在地生產的葡萄酒。我買了些新鮮蔬果，這個禮拜就不愁沒有營養的食材可煮了！如果你家附近有農民市集的話，我強烈建議去那裡逛逛。

參考解答

I went to a farmers' market on the weekend. It's a place where local farmers sell their produce directly to the public. There were loads of vendors offering an enormous variety of food that looked tasty and smelled delightful. I sampled some of my favorites—cheese and sausages—and also drank locally produced wine. I bought some fresh fruit and vegetables so that I have nutritious ingredients to cook with this week. If there's a farmers' market in your area, I highly recommend checking it out.

重要單字片語

- **produce** [ˋprodjus] *n.* 農產品（不可數）＆ [prəˋd(j)us] *vt.* 生產
- **load** [lod] *n.* 負載量　a load / loads of... 大量……
- **vendor** [ˋvɛndɚ] *n.* 小販
- **enormous** [ɪˋnɔrməs] *a.* 巨大的
- **delightful** [dɪˋlaɪtfəl] *a.* 誘人的；愉快的
- **recommend** [ˌrɛkəˋmɛnd] *vt.* 建議　recommend + V-ing 建議從事……

例 I recommend buying electronics manufactured in Japan.
我推薦購買日本製造的電子產品。

◉ 第二部分：英文作文

最近這幾年，許多企業紛紛投入發展人工智慧，也有許多人開始將人工智慧應用在生活中。請寫一篇文章

❶ 就你所知，使用人工智慧的好處與壞處分別是什麼？
❷ 你有在使用人工智慧協助你嗎？為什麼？

參考解答

I have read about artificial intelligence (AI) in the news a lot recently. It can process huge amounts of data very quickly. This can help us complete tasks more efficiently. However, it can make mistakes and generate false content. There are also privacy concerns, and some people are worried that it will take their jobs.

I have used AI at home to assist me with my homework. For instance, I asked ChatGPT to collect and summarize information for me when I was about to write a paper. This helped me process huge amounts of information quickly before I began writing. As long as I keep my own critical-thinking skills and do not rely on AI too much, it is a very useful tool.

近來在新聞裡面看過不少關於人工智慧的報導。人工智慧可以極快速地處理巨量資料。這可以幫我們更有效率地完成各種工作。不過人工智慧會犯錯以及產出不實的內容，況且也存在隱私權的問題，而有些人會擔心人工智慧搶走他們的工作。

我在家曾用人工智慧協助我做家庭作業。例如我要寫報告時，曾叫 ChatGPT 幫我蒐集與統整資

訊。這有助於我在開始撰寫之前先行消化大量資料。只要我仍保有我的批判思考技巧,不過度依賴人工智慧,它算是很有用的一種工具。

重要單字片語

- **efficiently** [ɪˋfɪʃəntlɪ] *adv.* 有效率地
- **generate** [ˋdʒɛnə͵ret] *vt.* 產生;造成
  例 The sales promotions generated huge profits.
  這些減價促銷活動獲利頗豐。
- **false** [fɔls] *a.* 不實的,假的
  a false name　　假名
- **summarize** [ˋsʌmə͵raɪz] *vt.* 摘要,總結
  例 Can you summarize the professor's lecture for me?
  你可以把教授的講課內容統整一下給我嗎?

口說能力測驗

第一部分:朗讀短文　150

　　Paul never really wanted to learn how to swim. He felt somewhat scared of the water and much preferred to stay on dry land. Nevertheless, his parents, believing swimming to be an essential skill, forced him to take lessons. While being monitored by a swimming instructor, Paul reluctantly got in the swimming pool for the first time. To his surprise, he loved every second of the experience. Even more amazingly, he discovered that he had a natural talent for swimming.

　　保羅從來就沒有很想學游泳。他有點怕水 ── 待在乾的陸地上好多了。然而他爸媽覺得游泳是很重要的技能,所以強迫他去上課學習。在游泳教練的監督下,保羅勉為其難地第一次下水進到游泳池裡。讓他感到驚訝的是,他竟然享受其中的每一刻。更令人意想不到的是,他發現自己有游泳的天賦。

重要單字片語

- **scared** [skɛrd] *a.* 感到害怕的
  be scared of...　　害怕……
  例 When I was very young, I was scared of dogs.
  我小時候很怕狗。
- **nevertheless** [͵nɛvɚðəˋlɛs] *adv.* 然而
- **force** [fɔrs] *vt.* 強迫
  force sb to V　　強迫某人做……
  例 Don't force me to do anything I don't want to do.
  不要強迫我做任何我不想做的事。
- **monitor** [ˋmɑnətɚ] *vt. & vi.* 監控
  例 The doctor will monitor the patient for two days after surgery.
  手術後的兩天內,醫生會密切注意這個病患。
- **instructor** [ɪnˋstrʌktɚ] *n.* 教練
- **reluctantly** [rɪˋlʌktəntlɪ] *adv.* 不情願地
- **discover** [dɪsˋkʌvɚ] *vt.* 發現
  例 The scientists have discovered a cure for the scary disease.
  科學家已發現治療此恐怖疾病的方法。
- **talent** [ˋtælənt] *n.* 天賦

　　Climate change is having a major impact on wildlife around the world. Some species are dealing with the loss of their natural environments. Polar bears, for instance, are reacting to melting ice by traveling longer distances to seek sources of food. Other species are experiencing changes in their natural cycles. Birds, for example, are arriving in their winter destinations too late for sufficient food to be available. This causes a chain reaction on other creatures in the food chain that depend on them.

　　氣候變遷正對全球的野生動物造成巨大的衝擊。有些物種正面臨天然環境的喪失。例如北極熊

TEST 4

為了因應冰雪融化而跑到更遠的地方去尋找食物來源。其他物種則正經歷自然週期的改變。例如有些鳥類太晚抵達過冬的地方而無法尋得足夠的食物。對於在食物鏈裡依靠這些鳥類的其他動物而言，這會造成連鎖反應。

重要單字片語

- **impact** [`ɪmpækt] n. 影響，衝擊
  have an impact on...　　對……有影響
  例 Andy's speech had a deep impact on all of us.
  安迪的演講對我們全體都造成深切的影響。
- **species** [`spiʃɪz] n. 物種（單複數同形）
- **experience** [ɪk`spɪrɪəns] vt. 經歷，體驗
  例 After losing my job, I experienced feelings of depression.
  失業後我感到非常沮喪。
- **destination** [ˌdɛstə`neʃən] n. 目的地
  a holiday / tourist destination　　觀光勝地
- **sufficient** [sə`fɪʃənt] a. 充分的，足夠的

◉ 第二部分：回答問題　🔊 151

❶ Do you think pets should be allowed in restaurants? Why or why not?
你覺得寵物可以帶到餐廳嗎？請解釋理由。

示範回答

① For many people, pets are part of the family, so why shouldn't they bring them to a restaurant? As long as the animals are well-behaved, I don't think it's an issue.
對很多人來說，寵物是家庭的一員，所以他們為什麼不該帶寵物去餐廳呢？只要寵物守規矩，我不覺得這是個問題。

② No, I don't think pets should be permitted in restaurants. Having animals around when humans are eating is not very hygienic. Plus, not everyone feels comfortable around pets.
我不認為寵物可以帶進餐廳。人吃飯時旁邊有動物，這不太衛生。況且並非每個人都能對寵物處之泰然。

重要單字片語

- **as / so long as...**　　只要……
- **well-behaved** [wɛlbɪ`hevd] a. 守規矩的
- **permit** [pɚ`mɪt ] vt. & vi. 准許，允許（三態為：permit, permitted [ pɚ`mɪtɪd], permitted）
  例 We are not permitted to smoke here.
  我們不能在此地抽菸。
- **hygienic** [haɪ`dʒɛnɪk / haɪ`dʒinɪk] a. 衛生的

❷ When was the last time that you did something challenging?
你上次做有挑戰性的事情是什麼時候？

示範回答

① I went on my longest, highest, and toughest hike last month, and I successfully completed it. I would describe that as quite challenging.
我上個月去健行的山路是最長、地勢最高、最難爬的一次，而我完成了。我會說這是夠有挑戰性的了。

② Recently, I taught my younger sister how to ride a bike. It was challenging because I had to be very patient and ensure she was safe.
我最近教我妹妹騎腳踏車。這事情的挑戰在於我得非常有耐心，而且還要確保她的安全。

重要單字片語

- **challenging** [`tʃælɪndʒɪŋ] a. 有挑戰性的
- **patient** [`peʃənt] a. 有耐心的

- **ensure** [ɪnˈʃʊr] *vt.* 確保（可接名詞或 that 子句作受詞）
例 Please ensure that all lights are switched off before you leave the office.
請確認在你離開辦公室前所有燈都關掉了。

❸ Do you think that everyone should know how to cook?
你覺得每個人都該會做菜嗎？

示範回答

① Yes. Knowing how to cook is essential. If you can't cook, then you'll always be reliant on other people and you'll struggle to look after yourself.
對。會做菜是很重要的。如果不會做菜，你就總得靠其他人，沒辦法自給自足。

② Not everyone is naturally talented in the kitchen, so they shouldn't be forced to learn how to cook. They can eat at restaurants instead.
不是每個人都有下廚的天分，所以不該強迫他們學做菜。他們可以去餐廳吃啊。

重要單字片語

- **reliant** [rɪˈlaɪənt] *a.* 依賴的
  be reliant on...　依賴 / 仰賴……
例 Despite the fact that he is thirty, John is still reliant on his parents.
儘管約翰卅歲了，他仍然依賴他的父母親。

❹ Your friend tells you that he or she is struggling to stay motivated in class. What would you say to him or her?
你的朋友告訴你他 / 她沒有動力上學。你會跟他 / 她說什麼？

示範回答

① I would say that I know it's difficult to stay motivated in class, particularly during boring subjects like math or science, but our school days won't last forever.
我會說我知道維持上課的動力是很難，尤其是數學或自然這類枯燥的科目，但學校生活不會延續一輩子，總會過去的。

② If a friend told me that, I would offer some practical solutions, such as trying to participate more or finding a personal connection to the topic being taught.
如果有朋友跟我這樣說的話，我會提供一些實際的解決方法，像是試著上課多舉手發言，或是在學科當中尋找跟自己有連結的東西。

重要單字片語

- **motivated** [ˈmotɪˌvetɪd] *a.* 有動機的，積極的
- **practical** [ˈpræktɪkḷ] *a.* 可實施的
- **solution** [səˈluʃən] *n.* 解決辦法；答案
  a solution to sth
  某事物的解決辦法；某事物的答案
例 The mayor came up with a smart solution to the problem.
市長想出一個解決這項問題的聰明方法。
- **participate** [pɑrˈtɪsəˌpet] *vi.* 參加
  participate in...　參加……
例 In order to participate in that competition, Wilson trained for one year.
為了要參加那項比賽，威爾森練習了一年。

❺ Would you prefer to create an item yourself or buy it ready-made?
你比較喜歡自己製作物品，還是喜歡買現成的？

TEST 4

TEST 4

示範回答

① I would rather purchase an item that was already made. For instance, buying a bookcase is much easier and more convenient than making one yourself.
我比較想買已經做好的物品。例如買一個書櫃比自己製作來得簡單方便多了。

② I would prefer to create the item myself. It would be much more rewarding, for example, to make picture frames or candles than buy them.
我較喜歡自己製作物品。例如親手做相框或蠟燭，這比買的更有意義。

重要單字片語

- **purchase** [ˈpɝtʃəs] vt. 購買
例 You should have purchased the tickets to the concert two months ago.
你兩個月前就該買演唱會的票了。

- **rewarding** [rɪˈwɔrdɪŋ] a. 值得的；有報酬的

❻ What is your idea of the perfect day? Describe it to me.
你心目中完美的一天會是什麼樣子？請詳細說明。

示範回答

① To me, the perfect day would revolve around a beach on a tropical island. I would wake up late, go swimming in the ocean, sunbathe on the beach, and eat delicious meals right there on the sand. That sounds like paradise.
對我而言，完美的一天都跟熱帶島嶼的沙灘有關。我會睡到很晚才起來、去海裡游泳、在沙灘上做日光浴，並且直接在沙灘上吃美味的一餐。這樣的生活有如天堂。

② My perfect day would consist of having brunch with my family, going clothes shopping with my friends, having dinner with my boyfriend, and then curling up with a good book at night. It might sound simple, but it sounds perfect to me.
我的完美一天會是與家人一起吃早午餐、跟朋友去服裝店血拼、跟男友共進晚餐，然後到了夜晚窩在床上看本好書。這聽起來也許很普通，但對我來說是完美的。

重要單字片語

- **revolve** [rɪˈvɑlv] vi. 旋轉；公轉
revolve around...
繞著……轉；以……為中心
例 Jenny's life revolves around her four young children.
珍妮的生活重心是她那四個年紀還小的孩子。

- **paradise** [ˈpærəˌdaɪs] n. 天堂；樂園

- **consist** [kənˈsɪst] vi. 由……組成（與介詞 of 並用）
consist of...　　由……組成
例 This dish consists of vegetables, meat, and spices.
這道菜是用蔬菜、肉和香料烹調而成。

- **brunch** [brʌntʃ] n. 早午餐（由 breakfast 與 lunch 兩字結合而成）

- **curl** [kɝl] vt. 使捲曲
curl up　　蜷臥

❼ What are some of the best ways you can think of to save money?
你能想到哪些省錢的好方法？

示範回答

① One way to save money would be to reduce unnecessary spending. This could include canceling your Netflix subscription and gym membership, skipping coffees from expensive coffee shops, and reducing the number of times you eat at restaurants each week.

省錢的方法之一是減少不必要的開支，包括取消訂閱網飛以及退健身房會員、別去貴鬆鬆的咖啡館買咖啡，再來就是減少每週去餐廳吃飯的次數。

② The best way I can think of to save money is to create a budget. Budgets allow you to monitor what you are spending, which can help you identify where to cut costs. You could do this on an Excel document or download an app.

我能想到的省錢妙招是製作預算。預算表可以讓你監控自己的開銷，有助於你找出可以撙節開支的地方。你可以用 Excel 文件編預算，或下載應用程式也可以。

重要單字片語

- **unnecessary** [ʌnˋnɛsəˌsɛrɪ] *a.* 不必要的
- **subscription** [səbˋskrɪpʃən] *n.* 訂閱
- **skip** [skɪp] *vt.* 省略（三態為：skip, skipped [skɪpt], skipped）
- 例 Jerry skipped lunch in order to get his work done.
  傑瑞沒吃午餐，在趕工作。
- **budget** [ˋbʌdʒɪt] *n.* 預算
  on a tight budget　　預算吃緊

❽ Would you rather take an online course or an in-person course?
你比較喜歡上線上課程還是實體課程？

示範回答

① I would prefer to take a course over the internet. That way, I could stay in the comfort of my home and possibly do it at a time of my choosing. It seems pointless to attend an in-person course nowadays.

我比較喜歡透過網路上課。如此我就可以待在舒適的家裡，也許還能自己挑時間上課。現在去上實體課程似乎很沒什麼意義。

② I would much rather take a course in person than do it online. I think interacting with fellow students and the teacher in real life is a vital part of learning. For instance, it makes it easier to ask questions.

比起上線上課程，我更喜歡上實體課。我覺得跟同學、老師實際互動是學習的重要元素。例如要問問題也比較容易。

重要單字片語

- **in-person** [ɪnˋpɝsn̩] *a.* 實際的，親自的
  in person　　實際，親自
- **pointless** [ˋpɔɪntlɪs] *a.* 無意義的
- **fellow** [ˋfɛlo] *a.* 同伴的

❾ Which skill would you most like to learn? Tell me about it.
你最想學哪種技能？請告訴我。

示範回答

① I would love to learn how to play the electric guitar. Possessing the skill to play this instrument would be a dream come true. I would then be able to start a band and perform on stage in front of thousands of fans.

我很想學彈電吉他。若擁有彈奏此種樂器的技能，那就是美夢成真了。我將可以創立一個樂團，然後在成千上萬粉絲前登臺演出。

TEST 4

⑨ One of my friends is a very talented painter. He creates beautiful landscape paintings and portraits that truly capture the character of the subject. If I had the time, I would like to learn how to paint just like him.
我有個朋友是天分極高的畫家。他畫的美麗風景畫與肖像畫真正捕捉到了題材的特色。如果我有時間的話，會想學習畫得像他一樣好。

重要單字片語

- **possess** [pəˋzɛs] *vt.* 擁有，持有
例 Peter's father possesses a good sense of humor.
彼得的父親很有幽默感。
- **stage** [stedʒ] *n.* 舞臺
on stage　登臺演出
- **portrait** [ˋpɔrtret] *n.* 肖像，畫像
- **capture** [ˋkæptʃɚ] *vt.* 捕捉；獲得
例 The car accident was captured by security cameras.
那場車禍已被監視器拍攝下來。

⑩ What do you usually do when you commute? Tell me about it.
你通勤時通常會做什麼？請告訴我。

示範回答

① When I commute, I usually listen to a podcast. I'm currently listening to a true crime podcast, which includes fascinating stories about unsolved cases. It's so interesting that I worry I may miss my stop and forget to get off the bus!
我在通勤時通常會聽播客節目。我目前正在聽的是有關真實刑案的播客，包含一些未破案的驚異事件。節目太有趣了，以至於我常擔心會坐過站忘記下公車！

② I tend to feel quite tired in the morning, so I just play a simple game on my phone that doesn't require too much thought. When I'm commuting home in the evening, I like to read a book or a magazine.
我早上通常感覺很累，所以只會在手機上玩不太需要動腦的簡單遊戲。傍晚坐車回家時，我喜歡看書或雜誌。

重要單字片語

- **commute** [kəˋmjut] *vi.* 通勤
commute from A to B
通勤於 A 地和 B 地之間
例 Tina commutes daily from her home to her office by car.
蒂娜每天開車通勤於她家和辦公室之間。
- **crime** [kraɪm] *n.* 犯罪案件，罪行
- **podcast** [ˋpɑd͵kæst] *n.* 播客（由 iPod 和 broadcast 拼綴而成）
- **get on / off a bus**　上／下公車
- **thought** [θɔt] *n.* 想法，思考

◉ 第三部分：看圖敘述　🔊 152

示範回答

The picture shows two women crossing a city street on a rainy day. They are both carrying umbrellas to shelter from the rain.

They are using a pedestrian crossing and have 25 seconds left to get to the opposite side. Behind them, a taxi is driving across, having doubtless waited until the pedestrians were safely out of the way. Other vehicles, including another taxi and a bus, are waiting to do the same. According to a recently revised law, pedestrians on the crossing have the right of way, and any vehicles that don't yield will be fined. The drivers of the vehicles need to stop for pedestrians before making the turn to proceed with their trip.

這照片顯示兩名女子正在雨天中過馬路。她們倆都有撐傘以免被雨淋溼。她們正走在行人穿越道上，走到對面的時間還剩二十五秒。在她們身後，有一臺計程車正駛過行人穿越道。這輛計程車無疑是等行人安全通過後才過去的。其他車輛，包括另一臺計程車與一輛公車，也在等待通過。依據最近修改的法律，人行道上的行人擁有路權，任何不禮讓的車輛將遭到罰款。汽車駕駛人需要在轉彎前先停車，讓行人通過後才能轉彎繼續行駛。

重要單字片語

- **pedestrian** [pəˋdɛstrɪən] *n.* 行人
  a pedestrian crossing
  行人穿越道；斑馬線
  = a crosswalk

- **across** [əˋkrɔs] *prep.* 越過
例 Be careful when you walk across the street.
  你過街時要小心。

- **cross** [krɔs] *vt. & vi.* 越過
  crossing [ˋkrɔsɪŋ] *n.* 十字路口，交叉口
例 Look both ways before you cross the street.
  過馬路前注意兩側。

TEST 4

31

GEPT 中級複試模擬測驗 第 ❺ 回　參考解答與翻譯

寫作能力測驗

◉ 第一部分：中譯英

艾蜜莉亞（Amelia）的鄰居臨時要去出差，於是拜託她在此期間幫忙顧一下他的狗狗。艾蜜莉亞想到要照顧另一個生命，感到有點惶恐，但她覺得該幫鄰居的忙，所以就答應承擔這個責任。接下來七天，她遛狗、餵狗，還跟狗狗玩。原本艾蜜莉亞並未期待會跟那隻狗產生感情。然而他們倆很快就成了最好的朋友。當艾蜜莉亞的鄰居回來後，她立刻就去領養了一隻小狗！

參考解答

　　Amelia's neighbor, who had to go on a last-minute business trip, asked her to take care of his dog when he was away. Amelia felt a bit anxious at the thought of taking care of another living being, but she agreed to take on the responsibility because she thought she should help her neighbor. In the following seven days, she walked the dog, fed him, and played with him. Amelia hadn't expected to bond with the dog. However, they became best friends very quickly. Right after her neighbor came back, Amelia went and adopted a puppy for herself!

重要單字片語

- **a business trip**　　出差
- **responsibility** [rɪˌspɑnsəˋbɪlətɪ] *n.* 責任
- **bond** [bɑnd] *vi.* 建立關係 & *n.* 關係
  bond with...　　與……建立關係

◉ 第二部分：英文作文

在博物館與美術館等地，一年四季都會有各類的展覽供民眾參觀，多多參觀展覽是個增廣見聞的好方法。請寫一篇文章

❶ 你喜歡參觀各類展覽嗎？為什麼？
❷ 你上一次參觀展覽是什麼時候？展覽的主題是什麼？

參考解答

　　Going to exhibitions is one of my favorite hobbies. I always check the news and social media for the latest exhibitions in town. Design exhibitions, for example, give me the chance to check out the latest ideas by local and international designers and discover new trends. Science exhibitions, meanwhile, provide me with the opportunity to learn about interesting topics.

　　An exhibition I went to recently featured the renowned Dutch artist Vincent van Gogh. Instead of being shown in the traditional way, his paintings were displayed on huge screens on the walls and the floor. This method allowed visitors to become immersed in the works of art. It was a unique and interactive experience that I will never forget.

　　參觀展覽是我最喜歡的嗜好之一。我一直都有看新聞跟社群媒體，查詢本地最新的展覽有哪些。舉例來說，設計展讓我有機會見識本地與國際設計師的最新點子，發現最新的潮流。同時呢，科技展也讓我有機會懂一些有意思的主題。

　　我最近去的展覽是知名荷蘭畫家文森·梵谷的作品。他的畫作並沒有用傳統的方式來展示，而是用牆面與地板的巨大螢幕放映出來。這種方式能讓參觀者沉浸在其畫作當中。這次獨特又有互動的體驗讓我難以忘懷。

重要單字片語

- **exhibition** [ˌɛksəˋbɪʃən] *n.* 展覽會
  be on exhibition　　展出中
  = **be on display**

- 例 The paintings will be on exhibition until the end of the year.
  這些畫作將展出到年底。
- **display** [dɪˋsple] *vt. & n.* 展示；陳列
- 例 The sacred scrolls were displayed in a special case.
  這些神聖的卷軸放置在特製的展示櫃中展出。
- **immerse** [ɪˋmɝs] *vt.* 沉浸，埋首於（本文為過去分詞當形容詞）
- **interactive** [͵ɪntɚˋæktɪv] *a.* 互動的，相互作用的

口說能力測驗

第一部分：朗讀短文　153

　　My dad used to be an Uber driver. However, he found that sitting down and driving all day was giving him health problems, particularly with his back. He therefore quit the job and concentrated for a time on exercising and strengthening his back. Many people remarked that he looked significantly younger and fitter. So, he decided to become a fitness coach and help others achieve their fitness goals through a wide range of training programs. He loves his new career!

　　我爸以前開過 Uber。然而他發現整天坐著開車讓他的健康出現問題，尤其是背部。於是他不再開 Uber，花了一段時間專注做運動，增強他的背肌。許多人說他看起來明顯年輕許多，體態也更好了。這麼一來，他就決定當健身教練，透過多種訓練課程幫其他人達成健身的目標。他很愛他的新事業！

重要單字片語

- **used to V**　過去經常（但現在不再）做……
- 例 I used to listen to music when I studied.
  我以前讀書時都會聽音樂。

- **quit** [kwɪt] *vt.* 辭（職）& *vi.* 辭職（三態同形）
- 例 I quit my job because I have to take care of my sick father.
  為了照顧生病的父親，我把工作辭掉了。
- **concentrate** [ˋkɑnsṇ͵tret] *vt. & vi.* 集中
  concentrate on...　專注於……
- 例 You should concentrate on what the teacher says.
  你應當專心聽老師所說的話。
- **strengthen** [ˋstrɛŋθən] *vt.* 鞏固，加強
- 例 Jeff lifts weights to strengthen his muscles.
  傑夫練舉重來增強他的肌肉。
- **remark** [rɪˋmɑrk] *vt.* 說，談到
  remark that...　說……
- 例 Harry remarked that John wasn't cut out for the job.
  哈利表示約翰並不能勝任那份工作。
- **significantly** [sɪgˋnɪfəkəntlɪ] *adv.* 大大地，顯著地
- **achieve** [əˋtʃiv] *vt.* 達成；達到
  achieve a goal　達到目標
- **career** [kəˋrɪr] *n.* 職業（尤指終身職業）

　　Florida and Taiwan are not typically mentioned in the same breath. The former covers around 170,000 square kilometers, is mainly flat, and has a consistently warm climate throughout the year. The latter covers 36,000 square kilometers, has many mountainous regions, and has a more varied climate with distinct seasons. Nevertheless, it is possible to identify some similarities between the two. For example, they both get hit by tropical storms, and they are both ideal destinations for seafood lovers and water sports fans.

　　一般不會有人把佛羅里達州與臺灣相提並論。前者面積涵蓋約十七萬平方公里，地勢大致平坦，而且終年溫暖如春。後者面積涵蓋三萬六千平方公

TEST 5

33

TEST 5

里，有許多山區，氣候較為多樣、四季分明。儘管如此，還是有辦法在兩者之間找到某些相似點。例如兩者都會受到熱帶氣旋的襲擊，而且都是海產老饕與水上運動迷的絕佳去處。

重要單字片語

- **typically** [ˈtɪpɪklɪ] *adv.* 通常；典型地
- **in the same breath** 同時提出相牴觸的事
- **consistently** [kənˈsɪstəntlɪ] *adv.* 一致地，始終如一
- **region** [ˈridʒən] *n.* 區域
- **varied** [ˈvɛrɪd] *a.* 各式各樣的
- **distinct** [dɪˈstɪŋkt] *a.* 有區別的；明顯的
- **identify** [aɪˈdɛntəˌfaɪ] *vt.* 辨別，認出

例 I knew it was Mark on the phone because I could easily identify his voice.
我知道打電話的是馬克，因為我能輕易地認出他的聲音。

- **similarity** [ˌsɪməˈlærətɪ] *n.* 相似之處（可數），相似（不可數）
- **tropical** [ˈtrɑpɪkl] *a.* 熱帶的

◉ 第二部分：回答問題 🔊 154

❶ Do you think it is healthy to use social media every day?
你覺得每天使用社群媒體是健康的嗎？

示範回答

① Providing that you don't use it *all day* every day, then yes, I think it's absolutely fine to use social media on a daily basis.
只要不是每天從早到晚都在用，那麼我的答案是肯定的，每天用社群媒體絕對沒問題。

② No, I don't think that is healthy behavior. Checking social media every day can leave you feeling negative and make you compare yourself to other people.
我不覺得那是健康的行為。每天都看社群媒體會讓你感到很負面，而且會讓你產生比較心理。

重要單字片語

- **basis** [ˈbesɪs] *n.* 根據，基礎
  on a daily basis   每天
  = every day

❷ Are you a persuasive person? Why or why not?
你是個說服力強的人嗎？請解釋理由。

示範回答

① Yes, I think I am a persuasive person. I often get my own way and convince my friends to do the activity I want to do.
是的，我覺得我的說服力不錯。我通常都可以頤指氣使，說服朋友做我想做的活動。

② I do not consider myself a persuasive person. I tend to go along with other people's desires rather than persuade them of the merits of my own.
我覺得自己沒有說服力。我習慣順應他人的願望，而不是說服他們我的做法有什麼好處。

重要單字片語

- **persuasive** [pɚˈswesɪv] *a.* 有說服力的
  persuade [pɚˈswed] *vt.* 說服
  persuade sb to V   說服某人做……

例 Dan tried to persuade his parents to buy him a new computer.
丹試圖說服他的父母買一臺新電腦給他。

- **convince** [kənˈvɪns] *vt.* 說服，勸服
- **merit** [ˈmɛrɪt] *n.* 優點

❸ Do you worry about climate change? Tell me why or why not.
你會擔心氣候變遷嗎？請解釋理由。

示範回答

① Yes, I do, and I think that we should all worry about it. It affects everyone on the planet, and we need to urgently reverse it.

參考解答與翻譯

會，而且我覺得大家都應該要擔心。氣候變遷影響地球上的每一個人，所以我們得趕緊逆轉這個現象。

② I know it's an important issue, but I don't spend time worrying about it. I am confident that technological advances will solve the problem in the future.
我知道這是重要的議題，但我不會花時間去擔心它。我對科技進步有信心，在未來會解決問題的。

重要單字片語

- **reverse** [rɪˈvɝs] *vt.* 扭轉，使反向；推翻
  例 Ian reversed the old photo to check if there was a date on the back.
  伊恩把這張舊照翻過來，看看背面有沒有日期。
- **confident** [ˈkɑnfədənt] *a.* 有信心的
- **advance** [ədˈvæns] *n.* 進步

④ Are you allergic to anything? How do you cope with the allergy?
你有對什麼東西過敏嗎？你怎麼面對過敏問題？

示範回答

① I have hay fever, so I am allergic to pollen. In spring, I get itchy eyes and a runny nose, so I try to stay indoors as much as possible.
我有花粉熱，所以對花粉過敏。春天時我的眼睛會癢還會流鼻涕，所以我會盡可能待在室內。

② Thankfully, I am not allergic to anything. I can eat seafood, nuts, and everything else without developing a rash or getting any other symptoms like that.
還好我沒有對任何東西過敏。我可以吃海鮮、堅果以及其他任何食物，並不會引發紅疹或是類似的症狀。

重要單字片語

- **allergic** [əˈlɝdʒɪk] *a.* 過敏的
  allergy [ˈælɚˌdʒɪ] *n.* 過敏
  be allergic to...　　對……過敏
  例 My son is allergic to pollen.
  我的兒子對花粉過敏。
- **cope** [kop] *vi.* 對抗，應付（與介詞 with 並用）
  cope with...　　處理……
  例 Vanessa finds it difficult to cope with stress.
  凡妮莎發現自己很難應付壓力。
- **hay** [he] *n.* 乾草
  hay fever　　花粉熱，乾草熱
- **pollen** [ˈpɑlən] *n.* 花粉
- **rash** [ræʃ] *n.* 疹子
- **symptom** [ˈsɪmptəm] *n.* 症狀

⑤ Is keeping up with the latest fashion trends important to you?
趕上最新的時尚潮流對你來說重要嗎？

示範回答

① Yes, fashion is very important to me. I like to look my best, and I am very interested in the latest collections in clothing stores.
是的，時尚對我來說非常重要。我喜歡精心裝扮，也對服飾店最新的時裝系列都很有興趣。

② No, not at all! Have you seen what I'm wearing? I would rather be comfortable than fashionable, and I don't care what fashion brands tell me to wear.
一點都不會！你看到我穿的衣服了嗎？我注重舒適遠超過時尚，也不在乎時尚品牌說我該穿什麼之類的。

重要單字片語

- **keep up with...**　　跟上……
- **trend** [trɛnd] *n.* 趨勢；潮流
  keep up with the trends　　趕上潮流

TEST 5

35

TEST 5

- **look one's best**
  打扮得體面，看起來很迷人
- **fashionable** [ˈfæʃənəbḷ] *a.* 流行的；時髦的

❻ Would you say that eating healthily or exercising is more important?
你會說吃得健康重要還是運動重要？

示範回答

① Both are important, but if I had to choose one, I would say exercise. If you have a big, unhealthy meal, for instance, you can try to work off all those extra calories by doing a lot of exercise.
兩個都重要，但如果非得選一個，我會選運動。例如你飽餐了一頓不健康的食物，還是可以用大量運動來消耗掉那些多的卡路里。

② In my opinion, what we put into our body is more important than exercise. There's a saying in English that goes, "You are what you eat." This means that our diet plays a major role in our health.
依我之見，吃下肚的東西比運動更重要。英文有句諺語說：「吃什麼長什麼。」這意味我們的飲食習慣在健康中扮演了重要的角色。

重要單字片語

- **work off sth** 擺脫……
  例 Jack works off his stress by playing basketball every day.
  傑克每天打籃球來減輕壓力。
- **calorie** [ˈkælərɪ] *n.* 卡路里

❼ Do you think that college students should take part-time jobs?
你覺得大學應該打工兼差嗎？

示範回答

① Yes, I think college students should take part-time jobs if possible. These jobs can help them pay off their student loans. Students can also learn how to juggle different responsibilities, which is a vital life skill.
是的，我覺得大學生有機會就該去打工。打工可以幫助他們還清學貸。學生也能學到如何同時兼顧不同的責任，這是很重要的生活技能。

② I think it is better if students do not take a part-time job. In college, they should be focused on their degree and achieving the best grades possible. A part-time job would distract them from these goals.
我覺得學生不要打工比較好。他們應該專心攻讀學位，把考試盡量考好。打工會讓他們分心，偏離目標。

重要單字片語

- **part-time** [ˌpɑrtˈtaɪm] *a.* 兼職的 & *adv.* 兼職地
  a part-time / full-time job 兼/全職工作
- **pay off...** 還清……
  例 How soon can you pay off the loan?
  你的貸款多快能還清？
- **loan** [lon] *n.* 貸款
- **juggle** [ˈdʒʌgḷ] *vt.* 同時兼顧
  例 The working parents tried very hard to juggle their family and careers.
  這對上班族父母努力嘗試兼顧家庭和事業。
- **degree** [dɪˈgri] *n.* 學位；程度，等級

❽ Do you think that there's still a gender bias in some industries? Why or why not?
你覺得在某些產業仍有性別偏見嗎？請解釋理由。

示範回答

① I think that there is a gender bias in industries such as engineering and finance. While more and more women are entering these fields, many of the leadership roles are still occupied by men. This is an issue that needs to be addressed.

我覺得在工程或金融等幾種產業裡面有性別偏見問題。越來越多女性進入這些領域，然而許多領導性的角色仍是男性在扮演。這個問題需要解決。

② There's been a lot of progress in recent years, so I don't think there is as much of a gender bias as there used to be. Nowadays, most managers and owners of companies want to employ the most-qualified person for the job, regardless of their gender.

近些年來進步很多了，所以我認為性別偏見的情況比以前少。現在大部分企業的經營階層與老闆會想要聘請最適任該職位的人，不會把性別列入考慮。

重要單字片語

- **bias** [ˈbaɪəs] *n.* 偏見
- **field** [fild] *n.* 領域；田野
- **occupy** [ˈɑkjəˌpaɪ] *vt.* 擁有（某職務）；占據（三態為：occupy, occupied [ˈɑkjəˌpaɪd], occupied）

例 Mr. Johnson occupies an important position in the government.
強森先生在政府裡身居要職。

- **address** [əˈdrɛs] *vt.* 解決（問題）

例 The government is trying to address the problem of unemployment.
政府正設法解決失業問題。

❾ How big of an impact does advertising have on your purchasing decisions?
廣告對你的購物決定有多大的影響力？

示範回答

① I think that advertising has a big impact on whether I buy things. If I see ads on social media, I often click on the links and end up buying products. In some cases, it's stuff I don't really need.

我覺得廣告對我要不要買東西有很大的影響力。如果我在社群媒體上看到廣告，通常會點擊連結進去看，結果常常就是買單了。有時候那個東西根本不是我需要的。

② I refuse to watch or listen to ads. It's just not something that I am interested in. If I want to buy something, I will do my own research before getting it. Advertisements don't factor into my decision.

我拒絕觀看或收聽廣告。我對它們沒興趣。如果我想要買某樣東西，會在購買前自行收集資訊。廣告不會成為我決定的因素。

重要單字片語

- **advertising** [ˈædvɚˌtaɪzɪŋ] *n.* 廣告（不可數）
  advertisement [ˌædvɚˈtaɪzmənt] *n.* 廣告（可數，常縮寫成 ad [æd]）
- **end up + V-ing** 到頭來做……

例 I believe that bad people will end up getting what they deserve.
我相信壞人終究會得到報應的。

- **stuff** [stʌf] *n.* 東西（不可數）
- **factor sth in / into sth**
  將……的因素考慮進……

❿ If you are feeling particularly stressed, what do you do about it?
如果你感到壓力特別大時，你會怎麼辦？

TEST 5

示範回答

① If I'm feeling stressed about my studies or something in my personal life, I talk about it with my friends. They help me to put things into perspective and find ways to deal with whatever is bothering me.
如果我的課業或個人生活當中有壓力，會去跟朋友吐露。他們會幫我從不同角度來看事情，並找到可處理我任何煩惱的解決之道。

② When I feel stressed, I do some vigorous exercise, like going for a run or doing a workout at the gym. These activities help to distract me from my worries and clear my mind. Plus, exercising releases chemicals that help lift your mood.
我感到壓力大時會做激烈運動，像是跑步或是去健身房鍛鍊等等。這些活動幫我暫時拋開煩惱，讓腦筋比較清楚。而且運動會釋放讓心情變好的化學物質。

重要單字片語

- **perspective** [pəˋspɛktɪv] *n.* 觀點
  put sth into perspective　　客觀地審視
- **vigorous** [ˋvɪgərəs] *a.* (體育活動) 劇烈的；健壯的
- **lift** [lɪft] *vt.* 舉起；解除
- **mood** [mud] *n.* 心情
  lift sb's mood　　使某人開心起來

🔊 第三部分：看圖敘述　155

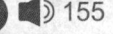

示範回答

In this photo, several people are walking along a narrow mountain path. They are obviously quite high up in the mountains, and there is a steep drop to their right. The hikers are all wearing helmets, holding onto a rope, and staying close to the left side of the path. All of this gives the impression that the route is potentially dangerous. I myself have been on several easy, low-level hikes over the years, but I have never participated in the activity shown in this photograph. I am concerned about developing altitude sickness, and I am a little scared of heights. Therefore, I can't see myself doing it any time in the future.

在這照片裡，有幾個人沿著狹窄的山路行走。他們很明顯在高山上，因為右邊的地勢很陡峭。這些健行客都戴著安全帽、手抓繩索、緊靠山路的左側。以上種種給人的印象是：這條路可能蠻危險的。我多年來也有去過幾次簡單、低難度的健行，但從沒參與過照片中顯示的這種活動。我會擔心得高山症，而且我有點懼高。因此我未來應該是不可能去參加圖中這種活動的。

重要單字片語

- **narrow** [ˋnæro] *a.* 狹窄的
- **route** [rut / raʊt] *n.* 路線
- **participate** [pɑrˋtɪsə͵pet] *vi.* 參加
  participate in...　　參加……
  例 Mary participated in the speech contest and came in third place.
  瑪麗參加演講比賽得了第三名。
- **altitude** [ˋæltə͵t(j)ud] *n.* (海拔) 高度
  altitude sickness　　高山症

GEPT 中級複試模擬測驗 第 ❻ 回 參考解答與翻譯

寫作能力測驗

◉ 第一部分：中譯英

傑洛米（Jeremy）第一次去巴黎的時候，以為可以光靠手機就能在市區各地趴趴走。他打算利用咖啡館和餐廳裡的免費 Wi-Fi 來規劃他從景點 A 到景點 B 的路線。然而他沒注意到他的手機沒電了，而他正在一處鳥不生蛋的郊區！於是他不得不轉換到替代方案：他得要去買一本地圖！

參考解答

The first time Jeremy went to Paris, he assumed he could rely solely on his smartphone to find his way around the city. He intended to use the free Wi-Fi in cafés and restaurants to plot his route from one tourist attraction to the next. However, he didn't notice that his phone was dead until it was too late, and he was in the middle of nowhere in the suburbs! He therefore had to switch to an alternative solution: he had to buy a map book!

重要單字片語

- **assume** [ə'sum] *vt.* 假定，認為
- **intend** [ɪn'tɛnd] *vt.* 意欲，想要
  intend to V   想要做……
- 例 Martin intends to major in economics when he goes to college.
  馬丁上大學後打算主修經濟學。
- **plot** [plɑt] *vt. & vi.* 計劃，圖謀（三態為：plot, plotted ['plɑtɪd], plotted）
- **route** [rut / raʊt] *n.* 路線
- **switch** [swɪtʃ] *vi.* 轉換（與介詞 to 並用）
  switch to...   轉換到……
- 例 I switch to a different channel whenever I see a political talk show on TV.
  每當我在電視上看到政論節目時，就會轉到別的頻道。
- **alternative** [ɔl'tɝnətɪv] *a.* 替代的

◉ 第二部分：英文作文

各地的城市有各自不同的特色與魅力，有些城市生活很方便，有些則非常有文藝氣息。請寫一篇文章
❶ 一個適合居住的城市需要有哪些條件？
❷ 你未來想要搬到哪裡住？

參考解答

A great city should have plenty of restaurants serving a variety of food. It should have a lot of entertainment options, from movie theaters and concert venues to museums and galleries. It must also have plenty of green spaces where you can escape the hustle and bustle of urban life. It also needs to have an efficient and reliable public transportation system.

In the future, I would love to move to Taichung. I think it checks all of those boxes: it has countless local and international dining options; it has the National Taichung Theater and the National Taiwan Museum of Fine Arts; it has tons of parks; and it has an impressive public transportation network.

適宜居住的城市應該有許多提供各式料理的餐館。它該有很多娛樂選項，從電影院、演唱會場地到博物館、美術館等等。它應該有大片綠地，讓人可以暫時遠離都市生活的喧囂。它也該有高效且可靠的大眾運輸系統。

我未來會想搬去臺中住。我覺得臺中符合上述的所有條件：它有非常多本地與國際美食的餐館可

TEST 6

39

TEST 6

選；有臺中國家歌劇院及國立臺灣美術館；有許多座公園，並且有很好的大眾運輸網路。

重要單字片語

- **plenty** [ˈplɛntɪ] *pron.* 充分（與介詞 of 並用）
  plenty of + 複數名詞 / 不可數名詞
  很多……
  例 We still have plenty of time to finish this project.
  我們還有很多時間來完成這項專案。
- **entertainment** [ˌɛntɚˈtenmənt] *n.* 娛樂，樂趣（不可數）；娛樂節目（可數）
- **venue** [ˈvɛnju] *n.* （舉辦）場所，地點
- **hustle and bustle**　　熙來攘往，忙忙碌碌

口說能力測驗

● 第一部分：朗讀短文　　156

I have to give a big presentation in class on Thursday. It's for history class, and it's about the civil war in the United States. This is a very interesting, emotional topic, and I have spent hours researching it online and in the library. My next task is to create a PowerPoint presentation that will impress my teacher as well as my fellow classmates. I will combine words and pictures to make it visually appealing. I am confident that I can get a good grade for this presentation.

這禮拜四我要在課堂上做重要的口頭報告。在歷史課上，我要講述美國南北戰爭的東西。這主題蠻有意思也蠻熱血的，我已經花了許多時間在網路跟圖書館裡蒐集資料。接下來我的工作就是要製作一份讓老師同學叫好的 PowerPoint 的投影片報告。我會結合文字與圖片，好讓投影片的視覺效果更佳。我自信這次口頭報告能拿到好成績。

重要單字片語

- **presentation** [ˌprɛzənˈteʃən] *n.* 口頭報告 / 簡報
  give / make a presentation
  做口頭報告 / 簡報
- **civil** [ˈsɪvḷ] *a.* 國內的；公民的
  a civil war　　內戰
- **emotional** [ɪˈmoʃənḷ] *a.* 感情激動的；情緒的
- **research** [rɪˈsɝtʃ] *vt.* 研究
- **impress** [ɪmˈprɛs] *vt.* 使印象深刻；使銘記
  例 Ted impressed me with his collection of various antiques.
  泰德的各式古董收藏相當精彩。
- **combine** [kəmˈbaɪn] *vt. & vi.* （使）結合
  combine A with / and B　　將 A 與 B 結合
  例 Maybe we should combine the plan with Jeff's idea.
  也許我們應該將這計畫與傑夫的想法結合起來。
- **confident** [ˈkɑnfədənt] *a.* 有信心的，確信的

It is no secret that climate change is causing the world's oceans to become warmer. This threatens the existence of tiny corals, which live in shallow waters and form colorful coral reefs. Now, scientists are breeding corals that are better able to resist warmer ocean temperatures. They have achieved this through a process known as selective breeding. However, the scientists have warned that this alone will not protect corals in the future.

氣候變遷正造成全球海水溫度升高，這已經不是祕密。它會威脅到生活在淺水海域、構建出繽紛珊瑚礁的小小珊瑚蟲的生存。現在科學家們正在培育能耐受較高水溫的珊瑚蟲。他們透過一種稱為選擇性育種的過程，且已經有了成果。不過這些科學

家仍警告大家說，單靠這樣的方式仍無法在未來全面保護珊瑚蟲。

重要單字片語

- **threaten** [ˋθrɛtn̩] *vt.* 威脅……

  例 The bank robbers threatened to kill the hostages if the police didn't agree to their demands.
  銀行搶匪威脅說若警方不答應其要求就將殺害人質。

- **existence** [ɪgˋzɪstəns] *n.* 存在
- **coral** [ˋkɔrəl] *n.* 珊瑚蟲（可數）；珊瑚（不可數）

  a coral reef　珊瑚礁

- **shallow** [ˋʃælo] *a.* 淺的
- **breed** [brid] *vt.* 繁殖（三態為：breed, bred [brɛd], bred）

  例 Some animals breed only at certain times of the year.
  有些動物只在一年中某些特定的時段才會進行繁殖。

- **resist** [rɪˋzɪst] *vt.* 耐（熱等）；抗拒 & *vi.* 抗拒
- **selective** [səˋlɛktɪv] *a.* 有選擇性的

🔊 第二部分：回答問題　157

❶ Do you prefer to brush your teeth first thing in the morning or after breakfast?
你比較喜歡剛起床就刷牙還是早餐後才刷牙？

示範回答

① I prefer to brush my teeth as soon as I get up. I want to get rid of the bad taste in my mouth when I wake up.
我比較喜歡一起床就刷牙。我想要去除起床時嘴裡的口臭。

② I like to brush my teeth after breakfast. That way, I can ensure that my teeth are clean before I go out for the day.
我喜歡早餐後再刷牙，這樣我才能確認每天出門前牙齒都是清潔的。

重要單字片語

- **first thing (in the morning)**
  （一大早）首要 / 馬上做的事情

❷ Should people always tell the truth? Why or why not?
人該永遠說實話嗎？請解釋理由。

示範回答

① Of course people should always tell the truth. Everyone should be truthful with other people in every part of their life.
人們當然該永遠說實話。每個人在生活各方面都應該對別人誠實。

② I don't think it's realistic to always tell the truth. Sometimes, the truth can do more harm than good, and a white lie would be better.
我覺得永遠說實話不太實際。有時候實話更傷人，善意的謊言還比較好。

重要單字片語

- **truthful** [ˋtruθfl̩] *a.* 誠實的
- **do more harm than good**　弊大於利
- **a white lie**　善意的謊言

❸ Which music genre do you prefer? Tell me about it.
你比較喜歡哪種類型的音樂？請詳細描述。

示範回答

① I love to listen to pop music. Pop songs are fun and have catchy lyrics. Listening to them makes me feel happy and positive.
我喜歡聽熱門音樂。熱門歌曲很有樂趣，而且歌詞都琅琅上口。聽的時候我會很快樂、很正向。

TEST 6

② Rock is my favorite music genre. I like the power and the passion of rock music, and the lyrics are often full of meaning.
搖滾是我最喜歡的音樂類型。我喜歡搖滾樂的力量跟熱情，而且歌詞通常都充滿意義。

重要單字片語

- **genre** [ˋʒɑnrə] *n.* 類型，體裁，風格
- **catchy** [ˋkætʃɪ] *a.* 悅耳易記的，琅琅上口的
- **lyrics** [ˋlɪrɪks] *n.* 歌詞（恆用複數）
- **passion** [ˋpæʃən] *n.* 熱情

❹ A friend tells you his or her favorite season is winter. How would you respond?
一個朋友告訴你他／她最愛的季節是冬季。你會怎麼回應？

示範回答

① If a friend told me that, I would say: "Me, too!" Winter is the best season because it provides a much-needed break from the roasting hot temperatures of summer.
如果朋友那樣跟我說，我會說：「我也是耶！」冬天最棒了，因為我們真的太需要從夏天炎熱的高溫當中解放一下了。

② I would tell him or her that I totally disagree. Winter is too cold. I much prefer spring or fall, when the temperatures are more pleasant.
我會跟他／她說我完全不苟同。冬天太冷了。我更喜歡春天或秋天，那時的氣溫比較宜人。

重要單字片語

- **roasting** [ˋrostɪŋ] *a.* 炙熱的；烤的
- **pleasant** [ˋplɛznt] *a.* 令人愉快的

❺ Do you think that students should be allowed to use calculators in exams?
你覺得學生考試時可以准許用計算機嗎？

示範回答

① Yes. Everyone has access to a calculator on their phones these days, so it makes sense to allow these devices to be used during exams.
可以。現在每個人手機上都有計算機可以用，所以考試時准許使用這樣的工具很合理。

② No, I don't think they should. Being able to do mental arithmetic without a calculator is a basic skill that everyone should possess.
我認為應該不准用。不用計算機就能心算是每個人應具備的基本技能。

重要單字片語

- **allow** [əˋlaʊ] *vt.* 允許，讓
  allow sb/sth to V　允許某人／某事物……
  例 That building is private property, and no one is allowed to go in.
  那是一棟私宅，任何人都不得進入。
- **calculator** [ˋkælkjə͵letɚ] *n.* 計算機
- **access** [ˋæksɛs] *n.* 使用；接近
  have access to...　使用……
  例 Students in that village do not have access to computers.
  那村子裡的學生沒有機會接觸電腦。
- **device** [dɪˋvaɪs] *n.* 裝置；設計
- **arithmetic** [əˋrɪθmətɪk] *n.* 算數（不可數）

❻ What is your favorite cultural tradition in your country? Please explain.
你最喜歡的本國文化傳統為何？請詳細解釋。

示範回答

① My favorite cultural tradition is the Mazu Pilgrimage. My family and I always join part of the journey. The atmosphere is great, and there is a real sense of communities coming together to celebrate the goddess of the sea.

我最喜歡的文化傳統是媽祖遶境。我跟家人都會去參與部份的遶境路程。遶境的氛圍很熱鬧，能真切感受到各社群凝聚在一起對這位海之女神的慶祝之情。

② I would say that my favorite cultural tradition in Taiwan is to have a barbecue on the Mid-Autumn Festival. It's wonderful to gather together with friends and family and celebrate the occasion with such mouth-watering food.
我會說我最喜歡的臺灣文化傳統是中秋節烤肉。與親朋好友相聚，享用香噴噴的食物一起過節，這種感覺最棒了。

重要單字片語

- **pilgrimage** [ˈpɪlɡrəmɪdʒ] *n.* 朝聖
  go on a pilgrimage　前往朝聖
- **atmosphere** [ˈætməs͵fɪr] *n.* 氛圍；大氣
- **barbecue** [ˈbɑrbɪkju] *n.* 烤肉聚會（可數）；烤出來的食物（不可數）（縮寫為 BBQ）
- **occasion** [əˈkeʒən] *n.* 特殊的大事；場合

❼ Could you tell me about a time when you learned from your mistakes?
說一個你從錯誤中學習到的教訓。

示範回答

① I remember a history exam I had to take a couple of years ago. History was by far my best subject, so I barely studied for it. However, the exam was really tough, and I almost failed. I have never made that mistake again.
我記得幾年前有一次考歷史。歷史是我最厲害的科目，所以我幾乎沒備考。然而那次考試超級難，我差點當掉。我從此沒再犯過同樣的錯誤。

② I used to take my best friend for granted. He was always there for me and listened to all of my problems, but I rarely showed that I appreciated his kindness. By and by we grew apart, and I didn't realize my mistake till it was too late. I still regret it today.
我曾把我最好的朋友視作理所當然。他總在我難過時陪著我，聆聽我所有的困擾，但我鮮少對他的善意表達感謝。我們漸行漸遠，而我知道自己犯的錯誤時已經來不及了。我到今天仍然會後悔。

重要單字片語

- **fail** [fel] *vt. & vi.*（使）不及格 & *vi.* 失敗
  例 Mike didn't study hard, and thus he failed the test.
  邁可沒有認真念書，所以考試不及格。
- **take (sb/sth) for granted**
  認為（某人 / 某事物）是理所當然的
  例 We tend to take natural resources for granted nowadays.
  現在我們往往將天然資源視為理所當然。

❽ If you were to move to a different country, how would you make new friends?
如果你搬到另一個國家去，你如何交新朋友？

示範回答

① I would join local clubs, such as a book club or a hiking group, in order to meet new people. If I'd moved to a country where people speak a different language, I would also think about attending a language exchange group.
我會去參加當地社團如讀書會或登山社等等，好去認識新朋友。如果我搬去一個語言不同的國家，我也會考慮去參加語言交換社團。

TEST 6

② The first thing I would do is join local Facebook groups to find out what events are taking place in the area. I would also download apps that could help me meet people with similar hobbies and interests.
首先我會加入地區性臉書社團好得知當地有什麼活動。我也會下載應用程式，幫助我認識嗜好或興趣跟我相同的人。

重要單字片語

- **exchange** [ɪksˋtʃendʒ] *n. & vt.* 交換
- **take place**　　舉辦；發生

例 A lot of outdoor activities will take place in the park tomorrow.
明天公園裡會舉辦很多戶外活動。

- **similar** [ˋsɪməlɚ] *a.* 相似的
  be similar to...　　與……相似

例 Luke's views on art are similar to mine.
路克對藝術的看法和我很相似。

❾ Do you think celebrities have a mainly positive or negative influence on young people?
你覺得名人對年輕人的影響主要是正面的還是負面的？

示範回答

① In my opinion, celebrities have a generally positive effect on young people. When we see famous people, such as sportspeople and singers, who have used their talents and worked hard, we feel inspired to be successful as well.
就我而言，名人對年輕人的影響一般來說是正面的。當我們看到運動員或歌手等名人善用其天賦並努力奮鬥時，我們會受到啟發也想見賢思齊。

② I think they have a mainly negative impact on youngsters. Too many celebrities these days do not actually have much talent. They just go on ridiculous reality TV shows to achieve fame quickly. This sends out the wrong message to young people.
我覺得他們對年輕人的影響主要是負面的。現在有許多名人不是真的那麼有天賦。他們只是去上了荒謬的電視實境秀而爆紅。這對年輕人傳達了錯誤的訊息。

重要單字片語

- **celebrity** [səˋlɛbrətɪ] *n.* 名人
- **ridiculous** [rɪˋdɪkjələs] *a.* 可笑的，荒謬的
- **fame** [fem] *n.* 名氣，名聲（不可數）

❿ What would you do if someone interrupted you all the time? Please explain.
如果有人總是打斷你的話，你會怎麼做？請詳細解釋。

示範回答

① If someone constantly interrupted me when I was talking, I would politely ask him or her to stop because it is rude. He or she may not be aware of the problem and might need a reminder. I myself am always careful not to interrupt people when they're talking.
如果有人一直打斷我講話，我會禮貌地阻止他/她，因為那樣很沒禮貌。他/她可能沒意識到自己的問題，需要人提醒。我自己則是一向小心不要去打斷別人的講話。

② If that happened, I would probably just ignore it and try to continue the conversation as best as I could. Everyone has annoying habits, and I would feel awkward having to tell them.

如果發生這種事，我可能會裝沒事，盡量讓對話繼續下去。每個人都有討厭的習慣，如果要跟他們說，我會不好意思。

重要單字片語

- **interrupt** [ˌɪntəˈrʌpt] *vt.* 打斷，中斷
- 例 It's impolite to interrupt others while they are talking.
  打斷別人談話是很不禮貌的。
- **constantly** [ˈkɑnstəntlɪ] *adv.* 一直，經常
- **ignore** [ɪgˈnɔr] *vt.* 忽視；不理會
- 例 Ben tried to be friendly to his new classmates, but they just ignored him.
  阿班對新同學示好，但他們卻不鳥他。
- **awkward** [ˈɔkwəd] *a.* 尷尬的

◉ 第三部分：看圖敘述　🔊 158

示範回答

　　This image shows a woman and a man in a bright, clean building. The woman is walking up the stairs, carrying a bag on her right arm and holding the handle of a small suitcase in her left hand. The man is a cleaner and is holding a dustpan and a broom. The two are making friendly eye contact, and the man may be offering the woman his assistance. I have been to places like this, such as hotels and apartment buildings, with bags and suitcases before. However, I have always chosen to use the elevator rather than take the stairs. If the elevator wasn't available, I would expect someone working there to help me with at least some of my bags.

　　這照片顯示一位女子與一位男子在一棟明亮、乾淨的大樓裡。女子正走上樓梯，右手臂上掛著手提包，左手則抓著小行李箱的提把。男子是清潔人員，手上拿著畚箕跟掃把。兩人正友善地對看，男子可能正要提供女子協助。我以前也曾經手拿包包、行李箱到過這類所在如飯店、公寓大樓等。不過我總是選擇搭電梯而不是爬樓梯。如果沒有電梯，我會希望那裡的工作人員能至少幫我拿部分的包包。

重要單字片語

- **dustpan** [ˈdʌstˌpæn] *n.* 畚箕
- **broom** [brum] *n.* 掃把
- **at least** 至少
- 例 Our target for this month is to produce at least 4,000 cars.
  我們本月的目標是生產至少四千輛汽車。

TEST 6

GEPT 中級複試模擬測驗 第 ❼ 回　參考解答與翻譯

寫作能力測驗

◉ 第一部分：中譯英

　　我向來都是個運動不行的人。我從來沒喜歡過學校的體育課，而且會刻意避免加入任何球隊。不過最近我發覺我很會跑。我跟幾個朋友在拼命跑要趕上捷運的末班車時，才意識到這個事實。我輕鬆趕上了車，但我的朋友全都沒趕上！這給了我自信，於是我就去練跑步。我現在每週跑三次，每次跑超過五公里。

參考解答

　　I had never been athletic. I never liked PE classes at school, and I avoided joining any sports teams on purpose. However, I recently discovered that I was good at running. I became aware of this when I was dashing with several friends to catch the last MRT train. I caught the train with ease, but all of my friends missed it! This gave me confidence, and I started to practice running. Now I run three times a week, and I run over five kilometers each time.

重要單字片語

- **dash** [dæʃ] *vi.* 衝刺
  例 Frank dashed to the toilet as soon as the film was over.
  電影一結束，法蘭克馬上衝向廁所。
- **confidence** [ˈkɑnfədəns] *n.* 信心

◉ 第二部分：英文作文

校園內的霸凌事件層出不窮，我們應該正視這個問題，讓校園成為學生快樂成長的地方。請寫一篇文章
❶ 你在學校曾遭遇過霸凌嗎？
❷ 你會怎麼解決校園內的霸凌問題？

參考解答

　　Personally, I haven't been bullied at school, but one of my close friends has. He struggled with schoolwork, so several smart students began to pick on him. They teased him by stealing his notebook and doodling on it, and they laughed at his answers to the teachers' questions during class. The situation made him very depressed and didn't stop until I stepped in and told a teacher about it.

　　If I were in charge of the school system, I would address the issue of bullying by raising awareness of the damage it can cause. This could be in the form of specific lessons that draw attention to the problem and give students a chance to talk openly about it. I think open communication in the school environment is key to stopping bullying once and for all.

　　在學校裡，我自己是沒有被霸凌過，但某個好友有過此經驗。他成績不好，所以有幾個聰明的同學開始找他麻煩。他們戲弄他，偷拿他的筆記本亂畫，還在他上課回答老師問題時譏笑他。這情形讓他感到非常難過，直到我介入去報告老師後才停止。

　　如果是我來管理學校，我處理霸凌問題的方式會是讓大家意識到它可能造成的嚴重傷害。我可以採用特別課程的形式，來引起大家對此問題的關注，讓學生有機會公開討論。我認為在學校環境中，誠懇的溝通是徹底杜絕霸凌的關鍵。

重要單字片語

- **bully** [ˈbʊlɪ] *vt.* 欺負，霸凌 & *n.* 霸凌者（三態為：bully, bullied [ˈbʊlɪd], bullied）bullying [ˈbʊlɪɪŋ] *n.* 霸凌（不可數）

- **pick on sb**　　找某人麻煩
例 The girl picked on Susie every day at school.
那個女生每天在學校都會找蘇西的麻煩。

- **step in...**　　插手……，介入……

- **once and for all**　　斷然，最後一次
例 John has quit smoking once and for all.
約翰徹底戒菸了。

口說能力測驗

第一部分：朗讀短文　　159

Liam was looking forward to a trip to the skateboard park with his friends. When he set off from home, though, he noticed that his elderly neighbor, Rose, was working in her garden. She seemed to be tired and struggling with the manual work. Liam knew he must offer his assistance; the skateboarding could wait. Despite Rose's initial refusals, Liam took over the gardening and allowed his neighbor to rest. He was soon rewarded with a beaming smile and a glass of ice-cold lemonade.

連恩滿心期盼著跟朋友去滑板公園玩。但他從家裡出來時，看到鄰居老太太羅絲在花園裡工作。她看起來很累，做不動這些粗活兒。連恩心知他應該主動幫忙。溜滑板沒有那麼急。雖然羅絲一開始說不要，但連恩還是接手了她的庭園工作，讓這位鄰居老太太可以休息。他很快就得到老太太報以燦爛的笑容以及一杯冰涼的檸檬水。

重要單字片語

- **set off...**　　出發……
例 Alice put her cat in the pet carrier and set off for the animal hospital.
艾莉絲把她的貓咪放在寵物籠裡，出發前往動物醫院。

- **elderly** [ˈɛldəlɪ] *a.* 年老的
- **manual** [ˈmænjʊəl] *a.* 手工的；用手操作的
  manual labor　　勞力工作
- **assistance** [əˈsɪstəns] *n.* 幫助
- **despite** [dɪˈspaɪt] *prep.* 儘管
- **initial** [ɪˈnɪʃəl] *a.* 開始的，最初的
- **refusal** [rɪˈfjuzl̩] *n.* 拒絕
- **take over...**　　接手……
例 When the director went on his honeymoon, Lucy took over his duties.
主管去度蜜月時，露西代他的班。

- **reward** [rɪˈwɔrd] *vt.* 報答，獎賞
  reward sb with sth　　用某物獎賞某人
例 The general rewarded the soldier with a medal.
將軍頒發獎章給這名士兵作為表揚。

- **beaming** [ˈbimɪŋ] *a.* 笑容滿面的
  a beaming smile　　燦爛的笑容

Western movies, which tell stories of life in the Old West of the US in the 19th century, often feature cowboys. However, the roots of the cowboy way of life stretch back as far as the 16th century. At this time, in what we now know as Mexico, Spanish colonists trained local men to ride horses and take care of cattle. As Spain expanded its empire across the southwestern part of North America, these cowboys did skillful and critical work that was also demanding and potentially dangerous.

西部電影講的是十九世紀美國西部拓荒時期的生活故事，裡面通常都會有牛仔。不過牛仔生活方式的源頭，最早可以回溯到十六世紀。當時西班牙殖民者在現在的墨西哥地區訓練當地男性騎馬及照顧牛群。在西班牙於北美洲西南部大肆擴張帝國版圖時，這些牛仔做的是技術性高且非常重要的工作，不但辛苦而且還可能會有危險。

TEST 7

TEST 7

重要單字片語

- **stretch** [strɛtʃ] *vi.* 延續；伸展
- 例 The investigation stretched over three years.
  這項調查歷時逾三年。
- **colonist** [ˈkɑlənɪst] *n.* 殖民者；殖民地居民
- **expand** [ɪkˈspænd] *vt. & vi.* 擴展，擴大
- 例 My father expanded the backyard to make room for a swimming pool.
  我爸把後院擴建，增加了蓋游泳池的空間。
- **empire** [ˈɛmpaɪr] *n.* 帝國
- **skillful** [ˈskɪlfəl] *a.* 技術性高的，熟練的
- **demanding** [dɪˈmændɪŋ] *a.* 費時費力的；苛求的
- **potentially** [pəˈtɛnʃəlɪ] *adv.* 潛在地

● 第二部分：回答問題 ▶) 160

❶ Could you tell me about a time when you helped someone?
描述一個你幫助別人的時刻。

示範回答

① This may not be an outstanding example of providing assistance, but I helped an elderly neighbor cross a busy road near our home yesterday morning.
這個例子也許沒什麼大不了的，不過我昨天早上有幫一個鄰居長者穿越我家附近一條車水馬龍的道路。

② One of my friends was getting very stressed about a geography exam recently, so I helped him to study and think more calmly about the situation.
我有個朋友最近為了考地理感到壓力很大，所以我幫忙他備考，讓他面對那個情況時較為平靜一些。

重要單字片語

- **outstanding** [aʊtˈstændɪŋ] *a.* 出眾的，傑出的
- **assistance** [əˈsɪstəns] *n.* 幫助
- **geography** [dʒɪˈɑgrəfɪ] *n.* 地理

❷ Do you collect specific items as a hobby?
你有收藏特定物品作為嗜好嗎？

示範回答

① I like to collect comic books and have built up a huge collection over the years. It would be great to own some first editions, but they're far too expensive for me.
我喜歡蒐集漫畫書，多年以來已經累積了大量的收藏。要是能有某些漫畫書的初版該多好，但對我來說那些太貴了。

② Yes, I collect action figures. More specifically, I collect figures from Japanese anime series, and I have a glass cabinet in which I keep them.
有，我收集公仔。說準確一點，我收藏的是日本動畫系列公仔，我有個玻璃櫃專門用來放它們。

重要單字片語

- **collect** [kəˈlɛkt] *vt.* 收藏，收集
  collection [kəˈlɛkʃən] *n.* 收藏
- 例 My little brother collects a lot of model planes.
  我弟弟收藏許多模型飛機。
- **specific** [spɪˈsɪfɪk] *a.* 特定的
- **an action figure**　公仔
- **anime** [ˈænɪme] *n.* 動畫片
- **series** [ˈsirɪz] *n.* 系列；(電視) 系列節目 (單複數同形)

❸ Would you ever consider taking public speaking classes? Why or why not?

你有考慮過去上個學演講的課程嗎？請解釋理由。

示範回答

① I am a self-assured public speaker. I know I've still got a lot to learn, though, so I would consider taking classes to help me get even better.

我是有自信的演講者。不過我知道還有很多東西可以學，所以我會考慮去上課然後變得更厲害。

② I don't like public speaking at all. The thought of taking a class in it terrifies me, so I would not consider signing up for one.

我一點都不喜歡演講。想到學演講就會讓我害怕，所以不會考慮去報名上演講課。

重要單字片語

- **self-assured** [ˈsɛlf əˈʃʊrd] *a.* 自信的
- **terrify** [ˈtɛrəˌfaɪ] *vt.* 驚嚇，使恐懼

例 Nick terrified his little sister with a ghost story.
尼克講鬼故事來嚇他的妹妹。

- **sign up for...** 報名……

例 Victor signed up for several computer courses to help him keep up with his co-workers.
維克多要讓自己能跟得上同事，於是報名了數種電腦課。

❹ What would be the first thing that you would do if you won the lottery?

如果你中了樂透，第一件事會做什麼？

示範回答

① If I won the lottery, the first thing I would do is throw a big party with all my family and friends to celebrate my good fortune!

如果我中樂透，第一件事就是開一個超大派對，跟所有親朋好友一起慶祝我的好運！

② The first thing I would do if I won the lottery would be to pay off my parents' mortgage. That would give them some financial security.

如果我中樂透，我首先會去還清爸媽的房貸。那樣做會讓他們財務自由。

重要單字片語

- **lottery** [ˈlɑtərɪ] *n.* 樂透，抽獎
  win the lottery　中樂透
- **throw** [θro] *vt.* 舉辦（= hold）& *vt.* & *vi.* 扔，擲（三態為：throw, threw [θru], thrown [θron]）
  throw a party　舉辦派對
- **fortune** [ˈfɔrtʃən] *n.* 運氣（不可數）；命運（可數）
- **mortgage** [ˈmɔrgɪdʒ] *n.* （不動產的）抵押貸款
  pay off a mortgage　還清房貸

❺ What are you prohibited from doing in your family? Tell me about it.

你在家裡被禁止做什麼事？請說明。

示範回答

① In my family, there is a rule that we cannot use our electronic devices, such as phones and tablets, during mealtimes. Instead, we must make conversation.

在我家有條規定，就是吃飯時不准用電子產品 ── 手機、平板之類的 ── 而是必須交談聊天。

TEST 7

② My father has a rule that no member of the family can get any tattoos or body piercings. He does not think they are appropriate.
我爸規定家裡任何人都不准刺青或是在身上穿洞。他覺得那很不得體。

重要單字片語

- **prohibit** [prəˋhɪbɪt] *vt.* 禁止
  prohibit sb from + N/V-ing
  禁止某人……
  例 Henry was prohibited from smoking in the lobby.
  亨利被禁止在大廳裡抽菸。
- **tattoo** [tæˋtu] *n.* 刺青
- **piercing** [ˋpɪrsɪŋ] *n.* 穿洞
- **appropriate** [əˋproprɪət] *a.* 適當的，合適的

❻ A friend asks about your most memorable childhood experience. What would you tell him or her?
有朋友問你最難忘的童年經驗。你會跟他 / 她說什麼？

示範回答

① I would tell him or her about the first time I went abroad. My parents took me to Disneyland in Tokyo when I was seven. Visiting the various attractions, like Adventureland and Fantasyland, was an exciting and unforgettable experience for me.
我會告訴他 / 她我第一次出國的事。七歲時爸媽帶我去東京迪士尼樂園。造訪不同的園區，像是探險世界、幻想世界等等，對我來說都是刺激又難忘的體驗。

② For my most memorable childhood experience, I would choose starring in the school play when I was eleven. I beat lots of my fellow classmates to the leading role, and everyone said I gave a great performance.
說到最難忘的兒時經驗，我會選十一歲時在學校話劇當主角的那件事。我打敗了許多同班同學才當上主角，而且每個人都說我演得很好。

重要單字片語

- **star** [stɑr] *vi.* 主演 & *vt.* 由……主演
  例 Robin Williams starred in many comedies as well as dramas.
  羅賓・威廉斯主演過許多喜劇及劇情片。
- **beat** [bit] *vt.* 擊敗（三態為：beat, beat, beaten [ˋbitn̩]）
  例 No one can beat John when it comes to singing.
  說到唱歌，沒有人比得上約翰。

❼ Try to imagine life if the internet simply disappeared. How do you think you would feel?
試著想像網路突然消失的生活。你覺得你會有怎樣的感覺？

示範回答

① I think I would feel lost without internet access. I wouldn't be able to do most of the things I take for granted, like contacting my friends, checking bus times, searching for information, or locating restaurants. It sounds like an absolute nightmare!
若沒有網路可用，我想我會很失落。我沒法做大部分我覺得理所當然的事情，例如跟朋友聯絡、查公車時刻表、搜尋資訊或是找餐廳的位置等等。沒網路會是個大災難！

② In some ways, I think it might be a relief. A lot of the bad aspects of the internet, such as negative social media, would no longer be a part of life. People managed for centuries without the internet, so I'm sure that people today would also adjust.
這在某些方面倒算是種解脫。許多網路上的負面因素，例如社群媒體裡的惡意，將不再是生活的一部分。人們多少個世紀以來都沒有網路也活得好好的，所以我相信現代人也可以適應。

重要單字片語

- **disappear** [ˌdɪsəˈpɪr] *vi.* 消失
  例 The magician disappeared in a puff of smoke.
  那位魔術師消失在一陣輕煙當中。
- **locate** [ˈloket / loˈket] *vt.* 找到……的位置
  例 The leader was unable to locate the meeting point on the map.
  隊長找不著標在地圖上的會合地點。
- **nightmare** [ˈnaɪtˌmɛr] *n.* 可怕的情景；惡夢
- **manage** [ˈmænɪdʒ] *vi.* 設法，順利完成
  例 How do you manage to keep your room so clean?
  你如何能把房間保持得如此乾淨？
- **adjust** [əˈdʒʌst] *vi.* 適應（與介詞 to 並用）
  例 Jason has adjusted to his new schedule.
  傑森已經適應了他的新作息。

❽ Do you ever use coupons to pay for items? Why or why not?
你有常用折價券買東西嗎？請解釋理由。

示範回答

① Yes, I often use coupons to pay for things, especially food and drink. If you can save some money on a product, why wouldn't you? Plus, it's very convenient these days to store electronic coupons on your phone.
有，我常用折價券買東西，尤其是吃喝類的。如果買東西能省點錢，幹嘛不省？況且現在把電子折價券存在手機裡是很方便的。

② No, I rarely use coupons to pay for items. If I want to purchase something, I will just buy it. Besides, it's a hassle to deal with lots of coupons and try to remember to use them.
沒有，我幾乎不用折價券買東西。如果我想買某樣東西就會直接去買。再說要處理那麼多折價券還要記得去用它們，真的很麻煩。

重要單字片語

- **coupon** [ˈkupɑn] *n.* 折價券，優惠券
- **hassle** [ˈhæsl̩] *n.* 麻煩，困難

❾ What is the best advice that you have ever received?
你曾經得到過的最佳忠告是什麼？

示範回答

① "Don't compare yourself to other people." That's the best piece of advice I have ever received. It made me realize that I don't have to be the fastest runner, the smartest student, or the most talented musician. I just need to concentrate on being myself.
「不要跟別人比較。」這就是我得到過最好的忠告。它讓我了解我不需要跑得最快、當最聰明的學生或是最有才氣的音樂家。我只要專心做自己就好。

TEST 7

② My uncle once told me that we need to work hard, but we also need to have fun. It's definitely important to study hard and be a good student, but there is much more to life than schoolwork.

我叔叔曾說，我們應該努力工作，但也要會玩。努力讀書當好學生固然重要，但生命中不僅只有課業而已。

重要單字片語

- **advice** [əd'vaɪs] *n.* 忠告，勸告，建議（不可數）
  a piece of advice　　一個忠告

❿ How important is it to you to spend lots of time outdoors?

對你來說，花很多時間待在戶外有多重要？

示範回答

① It's very important to me to spend time outdoors. Breathing in the fresh air and being in nature are vital to our well-being. That's why I try to go outside as much as possible. That could involve hiking in the mountains or simply taking a walk in the park.

對我來說待在戶外是非常重要的。呼吸新鮮空氣跟身處大自然，對我們的身心健康相當重要。所以我會盡可能走出戶外，或者到山裡健行，或者光在公園散個步也行。

② I am not much of an outdoor person. Most of my hobbies are indoor activities, such as playing video games, reading novels, and going to the gym. Therefore, spending lots of time outside is not particularly important to me.

我不算是熱愛戶外的人。我大部分的嗜好都是室內活動，像是打電玩、看小說跟上健身房之類的。所以花許多時間待在戶外對我來說不是特別重要。

重要單字片語

- **well-being** [ˌwɛl'biɪŋ] *n.* 安康，幸福（不可數）
- **take a walk**　　散步
  = go for a walk

◉ 第三部分：看圖敘述　🔊 161

示範回答

In this picture, a man is sitting by the side of a river. To protect himself from the sun, he is wearing a hat and sitting under an umbrella. On one side of him is a fishing rod, and on the other is a life ring. He is sitting on a cooler, which is used to store his bait and any fish that he might catch. My grandfather has taken me fishing a couple of times in the past. He finds the hobby to be rewarding and relaxing. However, I have to confess that I consider it quite boring. Sitting still for ages while waiting for the fish to bite and possibly catching nothing isn't something I would choose to do on my own.

參考解答與翻譯

　　在這張照片裡，一名男子正坐在河邊。為了防晒，他戴了帽子坐在陽傘下面。他身旁一邊是魚竿，另一邊是救生圈。他坐在保冷箱上，保冷箱是用來裝釣餌以及他可能會釣到的魚。我爺爺曾帶我去釣過幾次魚。他覺得這個嗜好很有成就感也很紓壓。不過我老實講，我覺得釣魚相當無聊。要長時間坐著不動等魚來咬餌，而且可能什麼都釣不到，這可不是我會想獨自去做的事情。

重要單字片語

- **rod** [rɑd] *n.* 棍棒
  a fishing rod　　釣魚竿
- **bait** [bet] *n.* 餌（集合名詞，不可數）
  take the bait
  （魚）吃魚餌；（人）上鉤，上當

TEST 7

53

GEPT 中級複試模擬測驗 第 ❽ 回　參考解答與翻譯

寫作能力測驗

◉ 第一部分：中譯英

我哥哥喬許（Josh）說他想在他生日那天早起看日出。我問他為什麼會有這種願望，他回答說他向來都睡很晚，從沒看過日出。於是在他生日當天，我們起了個大早，然後踏上通往公寓大樓屋頂的樓梯。我起初感到有點煩又很想睡覺，但當我看到喬許看著日出時臉上充滿了喜悅之情時，這些負面情緒就逐漸消失了。這是我與哥哥共享的美好時刻。

參考解答

My brother Josh said that he wanted to get up early on his birthday to watch the sun rise. I asked him how that wish came about, and he replied that he had always slept late and never saw a sunrise. So, on his birthday, we woke up early and ascended the stairs to the roof of our apartment building. I initially felt somewhat annoyed and sleepy, but when I saw the joy on Josh's face as he watched the sun rise, those feelings faded away. It was a wonderful moment I shared with my brother.

◉ 第二部分：英文作文

西諺有云：「滾石不生苔。」我們要時時保有求知慾、挑戰自己，讓自己去學習不同的新事物。請寫一篇文章
1. 請講述一個你嘗試新事物的時機點
2. 你學到了什麼？

參考解答

Last year, my mom put me in charge of cooking for the family. She and my dad both had to work late on a regular basis back then, so it made sense for me to take on the responsibility. Also, she thought it was an ideal opportunity for me to build up an important life skill.

At first, I felt quite stressed because I had never cooked before. However, over time, I gained a lot of confidence. I learned from scratch how to prepare, season, and cook a variety of ingredients and turn them into delicious meals. The experience also helped me develop multitasking skills, which enabled me to get several dishes ready at the same time.

去年我媽讓我負責給家裡煮飯。當時她跟爸爸都得工作到很晚，所以要我負起這責任算是合情合理。此外，她覺得這是讓我學習一項重要生活技能的絕佳機會。

起初我覺得壓力很大，因為我之前從來沒做過飯。不過時間久了後，我得到不少自信。我從零開始學習如何備料、調味、烹調各種食材，將其變成一道道美味佳餚。這經驗也幫助我培養出多工技能，讓我能同時做好好幾道菜。

重要單字片語

- **season** [ˈsizn̩] *vi. & vt.* 調味
  例 Mom seasoned the soup with a bit of salt.
  媽媽在湯裡加了點鹽巴調味。
- **same** [sem] *a.* 相同的
  at the same time　同時

口說能力測驗

◉ 第一部分：朗讀短文　🔊 162

Rodney is from the US. His first visit to Taiwan was defined by friendly people, delicious food, and world-class public transportation. However, Rodney also experienced some culture shock. He was surprised by the number of scooters that were parked on sidewalks. He was astonished by the sight of women carrying umbrellas to block out the sun. He was amazed that he didn't need to tip in any of the restaurants. And he was shocked to see so many people standing on only one side of the escalators!

羅德尼是美國人。他第一次來臺灣時，印象最深刻的是友善的人民、美食以及世界一流的大眾運輸。不過羅德尼也有體驗到文化衝擊。他很驚訝人行道上停了那麼多機車。他訝異於女性撐傘遮太陽的情景。在餐廳不用給小費也令他吃驚。他看到那麼多人都只站在電扶梯的同一邊更是大感驚奇！

重要單字片語

- **define** [dɪˋfaɪn] vt. 下定義，解釋；界定
  例 Wendy defines happiness as spending time with her family.
  溫蒂將快樂定義為和家人共處。
- **astonish** [əˋstɑnɪʃ] vt. 使驚訝
  be astonished at / by... 對……感到驚訝
  例 I was astonished at Shane's crazy behavior.
  我對尚恩的瘋狂行徑感到很驚訝。
- **tip** [tɪp] vi. & vt. 給小費 & n. 小費；尖端；祕訣
- **escalator** [ˋɛskəˏletɚ] n. 電扶梯

Nowadays, people lead very busy lives, and many struggle to fit a workout such as a long run or a swimming session into their daily schedule. However, recent research has shown that adding short bursts of exercise into our day can be just as beneficial for our physical and mental health. These "exercise snacks" can be as simple as ascending a few flights of stairs, taking a short, fast walk during lunchtime, or performing a few squats at your office desk.

現代人生活非常繁忙，許多人很難在日常作息裡安插進長跑或游泳等運動時間。不過最近的研究顯示，我們在一天中放進短暫而激烈的運動也能有益身心健康。這種「零食化的運動」可以簡單到像是爬幾層樓梯、午休時短暫快走，或是在辦公桌旁做幾個深蹲。

重要單字片語

- **session** [ˋsɛʃən] n.（某項活動的）一段時間
- **burst** [bɝst] n.（短期）增加，爆發；爆炸，噴；（感情）爆發
  a burst of laughter　突然大笑
- **beneficial** [ˏbɛnəˋfɪʃəl] a. 有益的
- **ascend** [əˋsɛnd] vt. 攀登 & vi. 上升
  例 The air became thinner as we ascended the mountain.
  我們爬上山時，空氣漸漸變得稀薄。
- **flight** [flaɪt] n. 一段樓梯
- **squat** [skwɑt] n. & vi. 蹲，蹲下

第二部分：回答問題　🔊 163

❶ Would you describe yourself as a morning person? Why or why not?
你會說自己是個早起的人嗎？請解釋理由。

示範回答

① Yes, without a doubt, I'm a morning person. As soon as the alarm goes off at 6:00 a.m., I immediately get out of bed and start my day feeling great.
會，我毫無疑問是早起的人。早上六點鬧鐘一響，我就會馬上起床，很有精神迎接這一天。

② I am the complete opposite of a morning person. My internal body clock wants me to go to bed late and get up late.
我完全不是早起的人。我的生理時鐘要求我晚睡晚起。

TEST 8

55

TEST 8

重要單字片語

- **internal** [ɪnˋtɝnl̩] *a.* 內部的

❷ Do you think that we rely on technology too much these days?
你覺得我們現在有沒有過份依賴科技？

示範回答

① While we definitely rely on technology a lot, I don't think we do it *too much*. It's there to be utilized, so that's precisely what we should do.
我們確實很依賴科技沒錯，但我覺得並沒有過份依賴。科技的存在就是為了被利用，而那正是我們應該做的。

② I do worry that people nowadays are too reliant on technology. It seems like most people can no longer read maps, do math in their head, or remember important facts.
我確實擔心現代人太過依賴科技。大部分的人似乎已經不會看地圖、不會心算也不記憶重要資訊了。

重要單字片語

- **utilize** [ˋjutl̩͵aɪz] *vt.* 利用
例 The power plant utilizes water to generate electricity.
這座發電廠利用水力發電。

- **precisely** [prɪˋsaɪslɪ] *adv.* 確切地
- **reliant** [rɪˋlaɪənt] *a.* 依賴的
A be reliant on B　　A 依賴 B

❸ Is there a food that you would like to eat but have never tried?
有哪種食物是你很想吃卻還未嘗過的？

示範回答

① I love pizza, but I've never had a proper Italian pizza. It would be a dream come true to travel to its country of origin and sample the real deal.
我愛比薩，但還沒吃過正宗的義大利比薩。要是能去比薩的發源地嚐嚐道地的比薩，就可算是美夢成真了。

② I've never tried sashimi. Part of me thinks eating raw fish sounds disgusting, but then another part of me wishes I were brave enough to try it.
我從沒吃過生魚片。部分的我覺得吃生魚聽起來很噁心，但另一部分的我又很希望能鼓起勇氣吃吃看。

重要單字片語

- **proper** [ˋprɑpɚ] *a.* 正確的，合宜的
- **sample** [ˋsæmpl̩] *vt.* 試吃；抽樣檢查
例 You are welcome to sample any flavor of our ice cream.
我們歡迎您試吃任何一種冰淇淋口味。
- **the real deal**　　極好的人事物
- **raw** [rɔ] *a.* 生的
- **brave** [brev] *a.* 勇敢的

❹ What would you say are some benefits of reading every day?
你覺得每天看書的好處是什麼？

示範回答

① Reading every day enhances your vocabulary. It also helps you to learn more about the world, increasing your knowledge of cultures other than your own.
每天看書可以增加你的字彙量，也可幫你更了解這世界，增長對其他文化的見聞。

② If we read books on a daily basis, then we spend less time on our phones. Every hour we spend away from a screen has got to be beneficial.
如果我們每天都看書，花在手機上的時間就會減少。遠離螢幕的每一個鐘頭都是有益處的。

重要單字片語

- **enhance** [ɪnˋhæns] *vt.* 增強
- 例 My teacher suggested reading English newspapers to enhance my vocabulary.
  我的老師建議看英文報紙來增加字彙量。
- **vocabulary** [vəˋkæbjə͵lɛrɪ] *n.* 字彙（量）
- **beneficial** [͵bɛnəˋfɪʃəl] *a.* 有益的

❺ Are you interested in art? Please tell me why or why not.
你對藝術感興趣嗎？請解釋理由。

示範回答

① Yes, I'm fascinated by art. You can tell a great deal about an artist and the period in which he or she was working even from a humble painting.
是的，我對藝術很著迷。就算是一幅不起眼的畫，你也可以從中辨識出關於該畫家的很多事情，以及他／她作畫的年代。

② I don't have much interest in art. Some of my friends like to go to art galleries and look at paintings, but I just do not understand the appeal.
我對藝術沒什麼興趣。我有些朋友喜歡去畫廊看畫，但我實在不懂有什麼吸引力。

重要單字片語

- **tell** [tɛl] *vt.* 辨別；講，告訴
- 例 Sally could tell that her boss was mad.
  莎莉看得出來她的老闆很火大。

- **humble** [ˋhʌmbl] *a.*（物）不起眼的，簡陋的；（人）謙虛的
- **gallery** [ˋgælərɪ] *n.* 畫廊，美術館
- **appeal** [əˋpil] *n.* 吸引力

❻ Do you think it's necessary to wear a watch nowadays? Why or why not?
你覺得現在還有必要戴手錶嗎？請解釋理由。

示範回答

① Yes, I do. Wearing a watch makes it very convenient to check the time so you're not late. Also, with smartwatches, people can do so much more than check the time; they can monitor their heartbeat and even check their oxygen levels.
我覺得有必要。戴手錶時看時間很方便，這樣才不會誤事。此外，智慧型手錶讓人們除了看時間之外，可以做的事情太多了：監測心跳，甚至可以測血氧。

② No, I don't think it's necessary to wear a watch these days. Everyone carries a phone around with them in their pocket, so if they need to check the time, they can just look at that device.
我不覺得現在還有戴手錶的必要。每個人不管到哪裡，口袋裡都揣著個手機，所以如果要看時間，看手機就好了。

重要單字片語

- **heartbeat** [ˋhɑrt͵bit] *n.* 心跳
- **oxygen** [ˋɑksədʒən] *n.* 氧氣

❼ Would you be happy to do a job that involved working lots of overtime?
你會樂意從事需要長時間加班的工作嗎？

TEST 8

示範回答

① If I were working in my dream job, doing something worthwhile that benefits society and gives me fulfillment, then yes, I would be happy doing lots of overtime. However, I should stress that I would expect to be paid for it!
如果我從事的是夢寐以求的工作：做有意義的事，對社會有貢獻又能讓我有成就感的話，那麼我會很願意常加班。不過要強調的一點是：我會要求加班費！

② No, that's the last thing I desire. I want to have a job where I can work hard for seven or eight hours but then leave immediately. I value my free time too much to spend unnecessary extra time in an office.
不會，我最討厭加班。我想要的工作是在我努力工作七或八小時後，可以馬上下班的那種。我很珍惜空閒時間，不會想花不必要的額外時間在辦公室裡。

重要單字片語

- **overtime** [ˈovɚˌtaɪm] *n.* 加班；加班時數 & *adv.* 加班
- **worthwhile** [ˈwɝθ(h)waɪl] *a.* 值得（做）的
- **fulfillment** [fʊlˈfɪlmənt] *n.* 成就（感）；實現
- **stress** [strɛs] *vt.* 強調
  例 Miss Wang stressed all of the key points again at the end of the class.
  王老師在下課之前再次強調所有的重點。

❽ Do you sleep like a log, or are you a light sleeper?
你是個睡得很沉的人還是個淺眠的人？

示範回答

① I sleep like a log. I'm a very deep sleeper: as soon as my head hits the pillow, I fall asleep and don't wake up for eight or nine hours. Having a dark, cool bedroom helps me achieve this.
我睡得很沉。我很好睡，只要頭一沾枕，就可以立刻睡著，八到九個小時後才會醒。暗暗的、涼爽的臥室有助於我一夜好眠。

② I wish I slept like a log! I'm a very light sleeper: any kind of noise wakes me up, from traffic in the street to someone getting up to use the bathroom. This means that I often feel tired in the morning.
但願我能好睡！我睡得很淺，任何噪音都能吵醒我，從馬路上的車聲到有人起來上廁所的聲音都行。這意味我早上通常都很累。

重要單字片語

- **log** [lɔg] *n.* 圓木
  sleep like a log　睡得很沉
- **asleep** [əˈslip] *a.* 睡著的
  fall asleep　睡著

❾ Are you an organized person? How could you become more organized?
你是個條理分明的人嗎？你要怎麼變得更有條不紊？

示範回答

① Yes, I am a very organized person. For example, when I'm studying for exams, I create a strict schedule that I follow religiously. There's always room to be more organized, of course. I could download some apps and create reminders to help me do this.

58

是的，我很有條理。舉例來說，當我準備考試時，會製作鉅細靡遺的進度表，並且嚴格遵守。當然，在條理這件事上永遠有進步的空間。我可以下載應用程式，設定提醒訊息等等來幫我更條理分明。

② I wish I could say I was organized, but I am not. My study desk is a mess, I am often late to appointments, and I regularly forget friends' birthdays. To be more organized, I could use the calendar app on my phone to record important events.

我希望能說自己是有條不紊的，可惜不是。我的書桌凌亂、約會常遲到，而且還時常忘記朋友的生日。若要更有條理，我可以用手機上的日曆程式來記下各種重要的事情。

重要單字片語

- **organized** [ˈɔrɡənˌaɪzd] *a.* 有條不紊的，有組織的
- **strict** [strɪkt] *a.* 嚴格的，嚴厲的
- **religiously** [rɪˈlɪdʒəslɪ] *adv.* 嚴加地，時常地；虔誠地
- **mess** [mɛs] *n.* 混亂
  be a mess　一團糟

❿ What are the characteristics of a good listener? Do you consider yourself a good listener?

好的傾聽者有什麼特徵？你覺得自己是好的傾聽者嗎？

示範回答

① You can tell that someone is a good listener when they ask you detailed follow-up questions about what you just said. It shows that they were paying close attention. I like to think that I put this into practice and can therefore be regarded as a good listener.

如果有人就細節部分追問你剛才說的話，你就知道那人是好的傾聽者。因為那顯示他們有在注意聽你說話。我多半覺得我有這樣做，因此可被視為好的傾聽者。

② A good listener pays attention to what the other people are saying instead of thinking about what he or she is going to say next. It's a surprisingly difficult thing to do, and I must confess that I don't do it very well.

好的傾聽者會專注於別人說了什麼，而不是在想自己接下來要說什麼。要做到這點意外地相當困難，我得坦承我不太在行。

重要單字片語

- **follow-up** [ˈfɑloˌʌp] *a.* 接續的，跟進的
- **practice** [ˈpræktɪs] *n. & vt.* （慣例）實行
  put sth into practice　　實行某事
  例 I want to put my idea into practice as soon as possible.
  我想將我的理念儘早付諸實行。
- **confess** [kənˈfɛs] *vt. & vi.* 承認，坦承
  confess + that 子句　　坦承……
  例 Julia confessed that she stole money from my wallet.
  茱莉亞坦承從我的皮夾偷了錢。

◉ 第三部分：看圖敘述　　🔊 164

TEST 8

示範回答

The photograph shows four people collecting trash at a campground. Two men are bending down and picking up polystyrene containers to place in a garbage bag. Two women, who are also holding several garbage bags, are walking somewhere. They are apparently cleaning up after themselves after camping. The four people are being responsible campers. It is common sense that we should leave no trash behind after a picnic or a camping activity. But many people ignore the rules and leave a mess, sometimes even causing disasters like forest fires. I would never want to be irresponsible like those people. My family and I always clean up the trash after we camp or have a picnic. I think that's the least we can do for the environment.

　　這張照片顯示四個人在露營地撿垃圾。兩名男子彎下腰來撿保麗龍餐盒放進垃圾袋。兩名女子也拿著幾個垃圾袋，看來正要走去哪裡。他們很顯然是在露營後收拾場地。這四人是有責任感的露營者。我們在野餐或露營後不應留下任何垃圾，這是常識，但許多人還是漠視規定，留下滿地狼藉，有時候甚至造成森林火災這樣的災難性後果。我絕不會像這些不負責任的人一樣。我跟家人在露營或野餐過後都會把垃圾收拾乾淨。我覺得這是我們能為環境所做的一點微薄貢獻。

重要單字片語

- **trash** [træʃ] *n.* 垃圾（不可數）
- **garbage** [ˋgɑrbɪdʒ] *n.* 垃圾（不可數）

GEPT 中級複試模擬測驗 第 ❾ 回　參考解答與翻譯

寫作能力測驗

◉ 第一部分：中譯英

亞伯特（Albert）覺得自己平日的穿著打扮有點乏味，於是決定改變造型。他跑去理髮店要求剪個新髮型，於是理髮師剃掉了亞伯特腦後與兩側的頭髮。亞伯特又選擇剃掉他留了十年的絡腮鬍，改成八字鬍。然後他跑去一間服飾店，買了各式各類的潮服與配飾。看來亞伯特是鐵了心要改變他的外貌了。

參考解答

Albert felt bored with his usual look, so he decided to change his style. He went to the barber's and asked for a new haircut. The barber shaved off the hair on the back and sides of his head. Albert also chose to get rid of his beard, which he had grown for a decade, and changed to a mustache. He then went to a clothing store and bought a bunch of fashionable clothes and accessories. It seems like Albert was really determined to transform his look.

重要單字片語

- **haircut** [ˈhɛr͵kʌt] *n.* 理髮
  have / get a haircut　剪頭髮
- **get rid of sb/sth**　擺脫某人／某物
  例 Remember to wash your hands to get rid of any germs.
  記得要洗手好殺死細菌。
- **beard** [bɪrd] *n.* 下巴及兩耳下方的鬍鬚
- **mustache** [ˈmʌstæʃ] *n.* 八字鬍
- **determined** [dɪˈtɝmɪnd] *a.* 有決心的
  be determined to V　決心要……
  例 I'm determined to quit smoking.
  我已下定決心要戒菸。

◉ 第二部分：英文作文

許多人在求學階段，最後往往會選擇就讀大學，以期望有更好的未來與就業機會。請寫一篇文章

❶ 請問你覺得讀大學的好處在哪裡？
❷ 你覺得每個人都應該可以免費上大學嗎？為什麼？

參考解答

　　Going to college helps young people become more independent. It expands their knowledge, encourages them to think critically, and allows them to meet new people. It can also help them to prepare for their future careers and give them a better chance of getting higher pay. However, I don't think a college education should be free for everyone.

　　There are several reasons for this. Firstly, the cost would be too much of a burden for taxpayers. Secondly, college is not suitable for everyone. Making it free would attract too many people who would otherwise be more successful in non-academic careers. Thirdly, if a college education were free, degrees would lose their value because everyone would have one. This would make it difficult for employers to eliminate job candidates during the recruitment process.

　　上大學能幫年輕人變得更獨立。大學能拓展知識、鼓勵批判性思考，還能讓他們交到新朋友。讀大學也能幫助他們準備投入職涯，且讓他們更有機會得到較高的薪資。雖說如此，我並不認為所有人都該免費上大學。

　　我的理由如下。首先，納稅人將難以承受如此的開銷。再者，大學並不是適合每一個人。大學免費會吸引太多本可在非學術領域職涯發光發熱的人

TEST 9

來就讀。第三點，如果大學免費，學位就會因為人人都有而失去價值。僱主在招聘過程中篩選求職者將變得很困難。

重要單字片語

- **critically** [ˈkrɪtɪklɪ] *adv.* 批判地
- **education** [ˌɛdʒəˈkeʃən] *n.* 教育
  higher education　　高等教育
- **taxpayer** [ˈtæksˌpeə] *n.* 納稅人
- **value** [ˈvælju] *n.* 價值
- **candidate** [ˈkændədet] *n.* 候選人，申請人

口說能力測驗

第一部分：朗讀短文　🔊 165

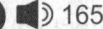

　　Tara loves reading novels, but she thinks that new books are too expensive. Therefore, she visits lots of second-hand bookstores to see if she can discover any novels that appeal to her. She found one the other day in a bookstore down an alley near her mom's office. The book was a fantasy romance. This wouldn't normally be Tara's cup of tea, but the reviews shown on the cover were so positive that she thought she should give it a shot.

　　泰拉喜愛看小說，但她覺得新書太貴了，因此她會造訪許多二手書店，看是否能找到吸引她的小說。前幾天她就找到一本，地點在媽媽公司附近小巷子裡的書店。那是本奇幻愛情小說。這種類型通常不是泰拉的菜，不過封面上的許多書評都相當推，所以她覺得應該給它一次機會。

重要單字片語

- **the other day**　　前幾天（與過去式並用）
  例 Carol bought a car the other day.
  　卡蘿前幾天買了一輛車。

- **alley** [ˈælɪ] *n.* 巷
- **be not sb's cup of tea**　　不是某人所喜歡的
  例 Romantic movies aren't Tom's cup of tea; he prefers action movies.
  　愛情片非湯姆所好，他比較喜歡動作片。
- **give sth a shot**　　試試看做某事物

　　Bonsai trees are tiny trees that are grown in pots. They are intended to resemble full-size trees and are carefully cultivated over years or even decades. This is achieved through cutting roots, using wires to direct branch growth, and changing pots every few years. The art of bonsai is primarily associated with Japan, where the skills of patience, imagination, and devotion required for the practice are highly regarded. It can be considered a perfect example of the harmony between humans and nature.

　　盆景是一種在花盆裡生長的迷你樹。它們通常會模仿原尺寸的樹的外觀，而且會被細心栽培好多年甚至幾十年。要做到維妙維肖，得透過修根、綁鐵線引導樹枝生長方向，且每幾年就更換花盆來達成。提到盆景藝術就會想到日本。在那裡，盆景藝術所需要的耐心、想像力與投入程度等技巧都受到高度的推崇。盆景藝術可視為人類與自然之間和諧共存的最佳案例。

重要單字片語

- **intend** [ɪnˈtɛnd] *vt.* 意欲，想要
  be intended to V　　目的是要……
  例 This medicine is intended to make me sleepy, but I'm wide awake.
  　這種藥本來是要讓我入睡的，但我卻非常清醒。

- **resemble** [rɪˈzɛmbl̩] *vt.* 像，與……相似
  例 It's weird that Sam doesn't resemble any of his family members.
  　奇怪的是山姆長得不像他家裡的任何一個人。

參考解答與翻譯

- **cultivate** [ˈkʌltəˌvet] *vt.* 培養
- 例 It is important to cultivate good habits.
  培養良好的習慣很重要。
- **primarily** [praɪˈmɛrəlɪ] *adv.* 主要地
- **devotion** [dɪˈvoʃən] *n.* 獻身，奉獻
- **harmony** [ˈhɑrmənɪ] *n.* 和諧

◎ 第二部分：回答問題　🔊 166

❶ Do you keep a journal? Please tell me why or why not.
你有寫日記嗎？請解釋理由。

示範回答

① Yes, I write in my journal every night. I use it not only to record my daily activities but also my deepest thoughts and fears.
有，我每晚都會寫日記。我寫日記不單是記錄日常活動而已，還會寫下我心底深處的想法與恐懼。

② I used to keep a journal when I was younger. Nowadays, though, my schedule is too full, and I don't have enough time to write in it.
我小時候曾經有寫日記。不過我現在的時間排滿滿的，沒空寫日記了。

重要單字片語

- **journal** [ˈdʒɝnl̩] *n.* 日記，日誌
  keep a journal　　寫日記
- **record** [rɪˈkɔrd] *vt.* 記錄
- 例 Can you please record what goes on at the meeting? I won't be there.
  你能幫我記錄一下會議的內容嗎？我不會出席。

❷ If you could have any job in the world, what would it be?
如果可以挑世上任何一種工作來做，你會做什麼？

示範回答

① I would really love to be a world-famous, Michelin-starred chef. Cooking is one of my passions, and I would like everyone to enjoy my culinary creations.
我真的很想當世界知名的米其林星級廚師。烹飪是我熱愛的事項之一，我想讓所有人都能夠享受到我烹製的菜餚。

② If I could have any job in the world, I'd choose to be a pilot. Everyone respects that profession, and pilots get to travel to cities all over the globe.
如果我可以做世上任何一種工作，我會選擇當機師。每個人都很尊敬這個職業，而且機師還可以環遊世界各個城市。

重要單字片語

- **chef** [ʃɛf] *n.* 廚師
  a head chef　　主廚
- **culinary** [ˈkʌləˌnɛrɪ] *a.* 烹飪的
- **pilot** [ˈpaɪlət] *n.* 飛行員；（船舶的）領航員

❸ Do you think that you handle criticism well? Please explain.
你覺得你能容忍被人批評嗎？請解釋理由。

示範回答

① If someone criticizes me, I think I am humble enough to accept it. I listen to what they say and try to adjust my behavior or actions accordingly.
如果有人批評我，我想我會虛心接受。我會聽他們說什麼，然後據此調整我的行為舉止。

② To be honest, no. I tend to be certain that I am in the right, so if someone challenges me or criticizes me, I find it hard to deal with.

TEST 9

TEST 9

老實說不能。我傾向肯定我才是對的一方，所以如果有人挑戰我或批評我，我會覺得很難接受。

重要單字片語

- **criticism** [ˈkrɪtəˌsɪzəm] *n.* 批評；評論（均不可數）
  criticize [ˈkrɪtɪˌsaɪz] *vt.* 批評
  例 The government was criticized for not taking the problem seriously.
  該政府因為沒有認真處理這個問題而受到批評。

- **accordingly** [əˈkɔrdɪŋlɪ] *adv.* 照著，相應地

- **be in the right**
  ……是正確的，……是有理的

❹ How often do you listen to music, and what device do you use?
你多常聽音樂，都用什麼裝置？

示範回答

① I listen to music the majority of the time. Whether I am studying, exercising, or commuting, I listen to music on my AirPods.
我大部分時間都有在聽音樂。不論是讀書、運動或通勤，我都會用 AirPods 耳機聽音樂。

② I listen to music on my phone occasionally, but usually I choose to listen to a podcast or watch videos on YouTube when I have spare time.
我偶爾會用手機聽音樂，不過我通常會在閒暇時選擇去聽播客或在 YouTube 上看影片。

重要單字片語

- **majority** [məˈdʒɔrətɪ] *n.* 大部分
  the / a majority of...　大部分的……

❺ Do you agree that parents should limit screen time for their children?
你同意父母應該限制小孩觀看影視螢幕的時間嗎？

示範回答

① Yes, I absolutely agree. I hate to see kids using tablets in restaurants when they should be engaging with their parents. Their screen time should be kept to a minimum.
完全同意。我很討厭在餐廳看到小孩在該跟父母互動的時候卻在玩平板。他們盯著螢幕看的時間應該被壓到最低限度。

② I think that is a decision for their parents. Also, we shouldn't assume that children are wasting their time on these devices. They could be doing something educational.
我覺得那該由他們的爸媽決定。此外，我們不該認定小孩使用那些裝置就是在浪費時間。他們也有可能是在看教育性的東西。

重要單字片語

- **engage** [ɪnˈgedʒ] *vi. & vt.* （使）從事
- **minimum** [ˈmɪnəməm] *n.* 最小量
- **assume** [əˈsum] *vt.* 假定，認為
  assume + that 子句　　假設……
  例 Rita didn't see Al wearing a wedding ring, so she assumed that he was single.
  麗塔看到艾爾並未戴著婚戒，所以她假定他還是單身。
- **educational** [ˌɛdʒəˈkeʃənl̩] *a.* 教育的；教育性的

❻ What are the best ways of making a good first impression on someone?
怎樣做最能讓人留下良好的第一印象？

示範回答

① Perhaps the best way to make a good first impression is to dress appropriately. For instance, if you are attending a job interview, you must dress formally in order to indicate to the interviewer that you are serious, responsible, and respectful.

得體的穿著或許最能製造良好的第一印象。例如去工作面試時，你就得穿正式一點，向面試官傳達你是認真、負責且尊重他人的訊息。

② I think a great way to make a good first impression on someone is to look them in the eye. Strong eye contact shows that you are confident in yourself and focused on the person you are talking to.

我認為眼神接觸是讓人留下良好第一印象的好方法。堅定的眼神接觸可顯示你對自己有自信並且專注在談話的對象身上。

重要單字片語

- **impression** [ɪmˋprɛʃən] *n.* 印象
  make a good / bad impression on sb
  留給某人一個好 / 壞印象
- **indicate** [ˋɪndə͵ket] *vt.* 顯示，表明
  indicate that... 顯示⋯⋯
- 例 This scientific research indicates that green tea can prevent cancer.
  這項科學研究顯示，綠茶可以預防癌症。

---

❼ An article you read says that recycling should be compulsory. What do you think of this idea?

你看過的某篇文章表示，資源回收應該是強制性的。你怎麼看待這想法？

示範回答

① Yes, I agree with the article that recycling should be compulsory. While most people do recycle, some lazy people do not. This latter group should be forced to recycle through fines or other punishments. It's the only way to make better use of our resources.

我同意文章所說資源回收應該強制的觀點。大部分人確實會做回收，但有些懶惰鬼不會。後面這類人應該透過罰款或其他處罰來逼他們做回收。唯有如此才能讓資源得到較佳的利用。

② I do not agree that recycling should be compulsory. Of course, it's essential for the sake of the Earth that we recycle, but people should be educated about the benefits and encouraged to recycle. They shouldn't be compelled to do so.

我不同意強制性資源回收。雖然我們為了地球而做回收的確是很重要，但人們應該被教導其優點然後被鼓勵去做回收。不應該用逼迫的方式。

重要單字片語

- **compulsory** [kəmˋpʌlsərɪ] *a.* 必須做的，強制性的
- **fine** [faɪn] *n. & vt.* 罰款
- **punishment** [ˋpʌnɪʃmənt] *n.* 懲罰
- **sake** [sek] *n.* 理由，緣故
  for the sake of... 為了⋯⋯的緣故
- 例 For the sake of everyone's safety, you should never drink and drive.
  為了大家的安全著想，你絕對不能酒駕。
- **compel** [kəmˋpɛl] *vt.* 強迫（三態為：compel, compelled [kəmˋpɛld], compelled）
  compel sb to V 強迫某人做⋯⋯
- 例 You can't compel me to do anything against my will.
  你不能強迫我做任何違反我意願的事。

---

❽ If you wanted to buy something expensive, would you use a credit card to pay for it?

如果你想要買某樣昂貴的東西，會用信用卡來付帳嗎？

TEST 9

示範回答

① If I really wanted the item, then yes, I would happily use a credit card to pay for it. Provided that I am confident I can make the repayments on the credit card, I see no reason not to use one.
如果我真的很想要那東西，那麼是的，我會很願意刷卡付帳。若我有自信可繳清信用卡帳單，沒理由不用它。

② No, I would save my money until I had sufficient funds to purchase the item I wanted. I would be too anxious about paying off my bill to use a credit card, and I would prefer to use one only for emergencies.
不會，我會存夠錢才去買我想要的東西。繳清帳單的焦慮感會讓我避免使用信用卡，我比較想只在緊急情況時才動用信用卡。

重要單字片語

- **sufficient** [səˋfɪʃənt] *a.* 充分的，足夠的
- **anxious** [ˋæŋkʃəs] *a.* 焦慮的
  be anxious about... 對……感到焦慮
  例 Nate was very anxious about his upcoming interview.
  奈特對即將到來的面試感到十分焦慮。

❾ Do you know your neighbors? Do you think it is important to know them?
你認識你的鄰居嗎？你覺得認識他們很重要嗎？

示範回答

① Yes, I know my neighbors quite well. They're mostly friendly, and we occasionally have gatherings in each others' apartments. I think it's good that we've become acquainted with our neighbors because it has brought a sense of community to our building.
認識；我跟鄰居們相當熟。他們大多都很友善，我們偶爾會在彼此的公寓聚餐。我覺得跟鄰居混熟蠻好的，因為這樣讓整棟大樓的人有了社區的認同感。

② I know my neighbors by sight, but I don't know their names or anything about their lives. My family and I prefer to keep to ourselves in the apartment building rather than socialize with the neighbors.
我認識鄰居的臉，但不知道他們叫什麼名字或是他們過著哪種人生。我跟家人在這公寓樓裡只想管好自己的事，不會想去跟鄰居打交道。

重要單字片語

- **neighbor** [ˋnebɚ] *n.* 鄰居
- **acquaint** [əˋkwent] *vt.* 使熟悉；使認識
  be acquainted with... 熟識……
  例 The two men are acquainted with each other.
  這兩個人彼此認識。
- **sight** [saɪt] *n.* 看見；視力（＝ eyesight）
- **keep to oneself** 不常與他人交往，獨處
- **socialize** [ˋsoʃə͵laɪz] *vi.* 交際，社交
  例 The old man hates to socialize with his neighbors.
  那名老人不喜歡和他的鄰居交際。

❿ If a friend invited you on a day trip to the zoo, how would you respond?
如果有朋友邀請你去動物園一日遊，你會怎麼回應？

示範回答

① I would respond with an emphatic yes! I'm a big fan of going to the zoo, and I like to learn about the fascinating and fearsome animals there. I would also confirm the details: who's coming with us, and when and where we are meeting.

我會大大地說聲好！我最愛去動物園了，我喜歡認識那些迷人又讓人怕怕的動物。此外我還會確認其他細節：誰會一起去、會合的時間地點等等。

② Zoos hold no appeal for me, so I would thank them for the invitation but politely decline. Of course, I wouldn't want the person to feel uncomfortable in this situation, so I would try to come up with a reasonable excuse for declining the invitation.

我對動物園無感，所以我會感謝邀約但有禮地婉拒。當然，我不想讓人家對此感到不快，所以我會想個拒絕邀約的合理藉口。

重要單字片語

- **emphatic** [ɪmˈfætɪk] *a.* 果斷的，堅決的
- **fearsome** [ˈfɪrsəm] *a.* 可怕的
- **confirm** [kənˈfɝm] *vt.* 確認
  例 Bill confirmed his hotel reservation two days before he went on his trip.
  比爾在出門旅行前兩天進行訂房確認。
- **decline** [dɪˈklaɪn] *vi.* & *vt.* 婉拒
  例 I offered to give Tina a ride home after the party, but she declined.
  派對結束後我提議載蒂娜回她家，但她婉拒了。
- **excuse** [ɪkˈskjus] *n.* 藉口

◎ 第三部分：看圖敘述 🔊 167

示範回答

In this picture, three people are wading through a rice field in a rural area. The rice paddy is wet and muddy, so they seem to be having difficulty moving in it. I assume that all of them are rice farmers and are in the middle of a day's work, and I can see that all the rice shoots are arranged neatly. I am fascinated by this kind of activity. Since a majority of people live and work in big cities now, they might have forgotten what traditional farming in the countryside looks like. I don't think I have the ability to do this day in and day out, but I would definitely like to give it a try. It would be very interesting to experience this way of life.

在這張照片中央的三個人正走在鄉村的稻田中間。稻田又溼又泥濘，因此他們看起來舉步維艱。我猜他們都是稻農，正在田間工作，我也看得出來所有稻秧都插得很整齊。我對這種事情蠻有興趣的。由於現在大部分人都在大城市裡居住與工作，他們可能已經忘記鄉間的傳統農業長什麼樣子了。我應該是沒這個本事日復一日做這個活兒，但我真的很想試上一試。能體驗一下這種生活方式一定很有意思。

重要單字片語

- **rural** [ˈrʊrəl] *a.* 鄉下的
  a rural area　　鄉村地區
- **shoot** [ʃut] *n.* 嫩芽，幼苗
- **day in and day out**　　日復一日

TEST 9

67

GEPT 中級複試模擬測驗 第 ❿ 回　參考解答與翻譯

寫作能力測驗

◉ 第一部分：中譯英

希臘是以歷史遺跡聞名的國家。所以當莎夏（Sasha）去那裡時，想要盡可能看到越多遺跡越好。在首都市區內，她造訪了山丘上的若干座古代建築物，其中一座是祭拜某位女神的神廟。她也跑去參觀了一個市集的遺跡，古代的人們會在那裡交易商品與觀看表演。莎夏對於所看到的一切都感到不可思議，決定未來還要再造訪這片土地。

參考解答

Greece is a country famous for its historical sites, so Sasha wanted to see as many of them as possible when she went there. In the capital city, she visited several ancient buildings on a hill. One of these structures was a temple devoted to a goddess. She also went to see the remains of a market where the ancient people traded goods and watched performances. Sasha was so fascinated by everything she saw that she decided to revisit the land in the future.

重要單字片語

- **structure** [ˈstrʌktʃɚ] *n.* 建築物；結構
- **devoted** [dɪˈvotɪd] *a.* 忠誠的；奉獻的
  be devoted to a god　祭拜某神明
- **goddess** [ˈɡɑdɪs] *n.* 女神
- **remains** [rɪˈmenz] *n.* 遺跡（恆用複數）

◉ 第二部分：英文作文

許多人長大後才有機會開始理財，而理財不單單只是儲蓄而已，還包含投資與預算規畫等等，我們從小就應該開始培養正確的理財觀念。請寫一篇文章

❶ 你認為學校應該教育學生如何理財嗎？
❷ 請說明原因

參考解答

Schools should definitely teach their students about managing their money. Skills such as budgeting, saving, and investing are a vital part of adult life. If children aren't educated about them, they may face serious problems in later years. For example, they may borrow too much money but not be able to pay it back. This could lead to more debts piling up, and they won't be able to afford a house or even a car. It may very likely hurt their relationships, too. Furthermore, they won't be able to save enough money for old age, which might leave them financially vulnerable once they retire. Learning about all of this at an early age will encourage them to develop responsible financial habits throughout their lives.

學校絕對應該教學生理財知識。諸如預算規畫、儲蓄、投資等理財技能都是成年生活中關鍵的一環。如果孩童時代沒學到這些，他們將來就可能面臨嚴重的問題。例如他們可能因過度借貸而無力償還。這可能導致債務累積到買不起房子甚至車子的境地，而且也很可能損害人際關係。尤有甚者，他們無法存錢防老，一旦退休就會陷入財務困境。早點學到這些觀念可以鼓勵他們終其一生養成負責任的理財習慣。

重要單字片語

- **financial** [faɪˈnænʃəl] *a.* 財務的；金融的
  finance [ˈfaɪnæns] *n.* 財政，財務
- **budgeting** [ˈbʌdʒɪtɪŋ] *n.* 預算規畫（不可數）
- **vulnerable** [ˈvʌlnərəbl] *a.* 脆弱的；（生理或心理）易受傷的
- **throughout** [θruˈaʊt] *prep.* 在整個……期間；遍及……

口說能力測驗

第一部分：朗讀短文 🔊 168

When Benny was 14, his parents considered him mature and capable enough to look after his younger sibling on his own. One night when they went out for a meal, they left Benny in charge of watching his sister, Diana. Benny felt a little anxious, but he rose to the occasion. He played games with Diana, gave her something to eat, made sure she had a bath and brushed her teeth, and then put her to bed. His parents were very proud of him.

班尼十四歲的時候，他的爸媽就覺得他已經成熟到有能力獨力照顧弟妹了。某天晚上當他們出外吃飯時，就讓班尼負責照顧妹妹黛安娜。雖然班尼有點緊張，但仍然勇敢面對。他跟黛安娜玩遊戲、給她吃東西、確認她有洗澡跟刷牙，然後送她上床睡覺。爸媽都為班尼感到驕傲。

重要單字片語

- **mature** [məˋtʃʊr] *a.* 成熟的
- **capable** [ˋkepəbḷ] *a.* 有能力的；做得出……的
  be capable of + N/V-ing
  有能力……的；可以……的
- 例 Don't worry. I'm capable of handling the problem myself.
  別擔心。我可以自己處理這個問題。
- **sibling** [ˋsɪblɪŋ] *n.* 兄弟姊妹（之一）
- **be in charge of...** 負責……
- 例 The manager is in charge of most of the administrative work in the office.
  該經理負責公司大部分的行政管理工作。
- **anxious** [ˋæŋkʃəs] *a.* 緊張的；焦慮的

Extreme heat events are on the rise around the globe, and they have the potential to kill. That is because when we're exposed to high temperatures for a long time, our body must work harder to cool down. We start to sweat, which can lead to dehydration if we don't drink sufficient water. This causes our heart to pump harder and can result in heat exhaustion, dizziness, and confusion. If our body temperature rises past 40°C, we can develop heatstroke, which is a medical emergency.

極端高溫的情況在全球越來越頻繁，而這可能是致命的，因為當我們長時間暴露在高溫中時，身體就必須花更大力氣來降溫。我們會開始流汗，而如果沒有攝取足夠水分的話，就會導致身體脫水。這會造成心臟更加劇烈跳動，進而導致熱衰竭、暈眩及精神錯亂。如果體溫超過攝氏四十度，我們就會中暑，在醫療上那就是緊急情況。

重要單字片語

- **be on the rise** 上升
- 例 Oil prices are on the rise.
  油價上漲中。
- **dehydration** [ˌdihaɪˋdreʃən] *n.* 脫水（不可數）
- **sufficient** [səˋfɪʃənt] *a.* 足夠的，充分的
- 例 We have sufficient funds to start a business.
  我們有足夠的資金可以創業。
- **exhaustion** [ɪgˋzɔstʃən] *n.* 筋疲力竭；耗盡
- **heatstroke** [ˋhitˌstrok] *n.* 中暑（不可數）

第二部分：回答問題 🔊 169

❶ Could you tell me about a time when you felt very lucky?
可以描述一次你覺得很幸運的時刻嗎？

TEST 10

示範回答

① On Lunar New Year's Eve, my entire family sat around a huge dining table, enjoying a delicious home-cooked meal, laughing and chatting. I felt really lucky to be part of that get-together.
除夕時,我們整個家族圍在一個超大飯桌旁享受美味的家常年夜飯,笑聲交雜著交談聲。我感覺能參與這聚會真是好幸運。

② I felt lucky when I won the top prize in a raffle at a charity event I attended. It was for a free night's stay in a five-star hotel!
我有次參加慈善活動,在抽獎時抽中了頭獎,我覺得超級幸運,因為頭獎是免費住一晚五星級飯店耶!

重要單字片語

- **raffle** [ˈræfl] *n.* 抽獎活動

❷ If it was raining outside, how would you spend your day?
如果外頭正下著雨,你會怎麼過這一天?

示範回答

① If I had to go out on a rainy day, I would just grab my umbrella and go out anyway. I wouldn't let rain affect my normal life.
如果必須在雨天外出,我會直接拿把傘頭也不回地出門。我不會讓下雨影響我的正常生活。

② I would take the opportunity to read a good novel, catch up on some TV shows, do some household chores, or simply get lazy and enjoy some "me time."
我會利用這個機會看本好小說、追一下電視劇、做點家事,或者乾脆耍廢享受一下「自己的時間」。

重要單字片語

- **affect** [əˈfɛkt] *vt.* 影響
- 例 The bad weather affected everyone's mood.
  惡劣的天氣影響了每個人的心情。
- **catch up on sth** 追上……的進度

❸ Have you ever filed a complaint? If not, what might make you complain?
你曾經客訴過嗎?如果沒有,什麼事情會讓你客訴?

示範回答

① Yes, I have. I filed a complaint when a package I waited for at home never arrived. The company gave me a full refund and a discount on my next order.
我有客訴過。我曾在家等包裹卻一直沒送來,我就去客訴了。那公司給我全額退款,且給我下一次訂購時可享折扣。

② I can't recall ever filing a complaint. However, I could imagine myself doing so due to poor customer service—for example, if a waiter or store clerk was rude or ignored me.
我不記得有客訴過。不過,我想像中的客訴應該會是針對很爛的服務,例如服務生或店員很沒禮貌或是不理我之類的。

重要單字片語

- **complaint** [kəmˈplent] *n.* 抱怨;投訴
  complain [kəmˈplen] *vt. & vi.* 抱怨
  file / make a complaint 投訴
  complain about + N/V-ing 抱怨……
- 例 Every time I see Christine, she complains about her job.
  每次我看到克莉絲汀,她都在抱怨她的工作。
- **recall** [rɪˈkɔl] *vt.* 回想,憶起,記得
  recall + N/V-ing... 記得……

❹ Do you think that you get a sufficient amount of sleep each night?
你覺得你每天晚上都有得到足夠的睡眠嗎？

示範回答

① Yes. I get around nine hours of sleep per night, which is recommended for my age group, and I wake up each morning feeling refreshed.
有。我每天晚上都睡九小時左右，是對我這種年齡的人推薦的長度，我每天早上起來都覺得很有精神。

② Unfortunately, no. It is often late by the time I have finished all my homework, so I only get around six or seven hours. Consequently, I feel tired most mornings.
很不幸，沒有。我寫完所有家庭作業時通常都很晚了，所以我只睡六到七個小時左右。因此我多數的早上都很累。

重要單字片語

- **recommend** [ˌrɛkəˈmɛnd] *vt.* 建議
  例 Muslims don't eat pork, so don't recommend this dish to Lena.
  穆斯林不吃豬肉，所以不要推薦這道菜給莉娜。

❺ Would you rather be a team leader or just a member?
你比較喜歡當隊長還是當隊員就好？

示範回答

① I would much rather be a team leader. I am confident and enjoy taking charge, so I like to be the one who makes the decisions.
我比較喜歡當隊長。我很有自信，而且喜歡當老大，所以想要當做決定的人。

② I would prefer to be just a member rather than the leader. I don't like the pressure or responsibility of being the person in charge.
我比較喜歡當個隊員就好而不是隊長。我不喜歡當老大要承擔的壓力跟責任。

重要單字片語

- **charge** [tʃɑrdʒ] *n.* 負責
  take charge of... 負責管理……
  = be in charge of...
  例 Sandy will take charge of the project while I'm in Hong Kong for the week.
  我去香港那個禮拜時，珊蒂會負責此專案。

❻ When was the last time you took time off due to illness? Tell me about it.
你上一次請病假是什麼時候？請詳細說明。

示範回答

① I took time off school a couple of years ago when I caught the flu. The illness really took its toll on me. I missed over a week's worth of classes, and it was very difficult to catch up.
我兩年前得流感時向學校請假。那次生病對我影響很大。我超過一整個禮拜沒有上課，要跟上進度非常困難。

② I took sick leave from work earlier this year. I was involved in a car accident and hurt my leg. It wasn't too serious, but I still needed a couple of days to recover. My colleagues looked after my work while I was absent.
我今年稍早有請病假沒去上班。我出車禍腿受傷。雖然沒有很嚴重，但我仍然需要幾天來養傷。我不在時同事代理我的工作。

TEST 10

重要單字片語

- **toll** [tol] *n.* 傷亡人數；過路費
  take its / a toll on sb　　對某人造成損害
- **recover** [rɪˋkʌvɚ] *vi.* 恢復
  recover from...　　從……康復
- 例 Some patients recover from cancer, so don't lose hope.
  有些病患的癌症會好，所以不要絕望。
- **colleague** [ˋkɑlig] *n.* 同事
- **absent** [ˋæbsn̩t] *a.* 缺席的；缺乏的

❼ Should it be mandatory to vote in elections? Why or why not?
選舉時應該強制大家去投票嗎？請解釋理由。

示範回答

① I think that making voting in elections mandatory is a very good idea. This policy would ensure that people became much more politically aware. It would also guarantee that the government was truly representative of the people.
我認為選舉時強制去投票是很好的想法。這個政策能讓民眾變得更關切政治，也能保證政府能真正代表人民。

② No, voting shouldn't be mandatory. Democracy means the right to choose, but it also means the right to choose *not* to be involved in the process. Besides, if people are forced to vote, they might begin to dislike the whole idea of democracy.
不應該。投票不該是強制性的。民主賦予我們選擇權，但也給我們不參與民主程序的權利。再者，如果民眾被迫去投票，他們可能會開始討厭民主這個概念。

重要單字片語

- **mandatory** [ˋmændə͵tɔrɪ] *a.* 強制的，義務的
- **aware** [əˋwɛr] *a.* 知道的；察覺的
- **guarantee** [͵gærənˋti] *vt.* 保證，擔保
- 例 I guarantee the price of this cell phone is the best deal you can find.
  我保證這支手機的優惠價格在別處是找不到的。
- **representative** [͵rɛprɪˋzɛntətɪv] *a.* 代表性的
- **democracy** [dɪˋmɑkrəsɪ] *n.* 民主（不可數）；民主國家（可數）

❽ How would you advise a friend or family member to be more environmentally friendly?
你要怎麼規勸朋友或家人更環保一點？

示範回答

① I would advise them to use their car as little as possible in order to reduce carbon emissions. Instead, they should walk, cycle, or use public transportation. They should also make sure to turn off electronic equipment when they are not using it to reduce energy consumption.
我會勸他們盡量少開車以減少碳排放，代之以步行、騎腳踏車，或是使用大眾交通工具。他們也一定要在沒使用電子設備時關閉電源，以減少能源消耗。

② If they want to reduce their carbon footprint, they can eat less meat and more vegetables. When shopping for groceries, they can focus on buying seasonal produce grown locally rather than transported halfway around the world.

如果他們想減少碳足跡，可以少吃肉、多吃蔬菜。去買菜時可以注意只買當令的本地農產品，而不是繞了大半地球運送過來的產品。

重要單字片語

- **environmentally** [ɪn͵vaɪrən`mɛntəlɪ] *adv.* 和環境有關地
  environmentally friendly　環保的
- **carbon** [`kɑrbən] *n.* 碳
- **emission** [ɪ`mɪʃən] *n.* （氣體、光線等）排放
  carbon emissions　碳排放
- **transportation** [͵trænspɚ`teʃən] *n.* 交通運輸（工具）（不可數）
  transport [træns`pɔrt] *vt.* 運輸
- **footprint** [`fʊt͵prɪnt] *n.* 足跡，腳印

⑨ Do you prefer to eat alone or with others? Please explain your answer.
你比較喜歡一個人吃飯還是跟別人一起吃飯？請解釋理由。

示範回答

① I prefer to eat alone. That way, I can choose which restaurant to go to, what to eat, and how long to spend there. I can also catch up on some reading or use my phone without worrying about engaging other people in conversation.
我比較喜歡一個人吃飯。這樣我才能選擇吃哪家、吃什麼，以及要在餐廳待多久。我也可以看點該看的書或是玩手機，不必記掛著要跟別人交談。

② I much prefer eating with other people to eating alone. Eating meals is about more than consuming food; it's about getting together with friends and family to laugh, chat, and connect with one another. Meals should always be social occasions.

我比較喜歡跟人一起吃飯，遠勝過一個人吃。吃飯不只是吃而已；跟親朋好友相聚歡笑、聊天、相互交流，那才叫做吃飯。吃飯一向都是有社交功能的。

⑩ Do you subscribe to any publications? Do you think that it is worth doing?
你有訂閱任何出版品嗎？你認為值得嗎？

示範回答

① Yes, I subscribe to *National Geographic*. It's full of educational content about the environment, animals, science, and space, and it features fantastic photography. I have an annual subscription, and in my opinion, it is definitely worth the money.
我有訂閱《國家地理》雜誌。它裡面的內容都是有關環境、動物、科學與太空等具有教育意義的內容，而且還有非常優質的照片。我每年訂一次，就我而言，這錢絕對花得值得。

② No, I don't subscribe to any publications. I can see the appeal if you are particularly interested in a topic and want to investigate it in depth. But I prefer to read articles online for free rather than pay a subscription fee.
我沒有訂閱任何刊物。我理解有人會對某種主題特別感興趣，想深入探索該領域。但我比較喜歡看免費的網路文章，不想付費訂閱。

重要單字片語

- **subscribe** [səb`skraɪb] *vi.* 訂閱
  subscription [səb`skrɪpʃən] *n.* 訂閱
  subscribe to sth　訂閱某（刊）物
  例 Lily subscribes to fashion magazines so she can keep up with the latest trends.
  莉莉訂閱時尚雜誌，以跟上最新潮流。
- **publication** [͵pʌblɪ`keʃən] *n.* 刊物

TEST 10

TEST 10

- **content** [ˈkɑntɛnt] *n.* （書、演講的）內容（不可數）；內容物（恆用複數）
- **investigate** [ɪnˈvɛstəˌɡet] *vt.* 調查
  例 The mayor promised to investigate the scandal.
  市長承諾會調查那樁醜聞。

◆ 第三部分：看圖敘述 🔊 170

示範回答

　　This photo shows a woman eating lunch at her desk while looking at her laptop. She is in a very nice office, but she obviously has too much work to do. Otherwise, she would be eating in a restaurant with her colleagues. Her meal, which seems to be fried chicken and a cup of bubble milk tea, looks delicious but unhealthy. It's not an issue if she only does this occasionally. However, if having a bento with a sweet drink at her desk while working happens on a daily basis, I reckon she might have a problem. It is important that people take a break from work. During their lunch break, office workers should get out of the office, take some exercise, and choose a healthy meal.

　　這張照片顯示一個在辦公桌前邊吃飯邊看筆電的女子。她的辦公室相當不錯，但她顯然是工作太多而做不完，否則她應該跟同事一起去餐廳吃飯才對。她的飯似乎包含炸雞跟一杯珍珠奶茶，看起來很好吃但並不健康。如果她只是偶而這樣吃，那麼問題不大。但如果在辦公桌前邊工作邊吃便當加糖份飲料是她的日常的話，我認為她可能會出問題。人們工作時短暫休息一下是很重要的。上班族在午休期間應該走出辦公室、活動活動，並且選健康的東西來吃。

重要單字片語

- **otherwise** [ˈʌðɚˌwaɪz] *adv.* 否則；以相反的方式
  例 Anita has to work over the weekend. Otherwise, she won't make her deadline.
  安妮塔這個週末得加班，否則她沒辦法如期把工作完成。
- **issue** [ˈɪʃjʊ] *n.* 問題，議題

國家圖書館出版品預行編目（CIP）資料

準！GEPT全民英檢中級複試10回高分模擬試題＋翻譯解答（寫作＆口說）：翻譯解答本／賴世雄作. -- 初版. -- 臺北市：常春藤數位出版股份有限公司, 2025.02
面； 公分. --（常春藤全民英檢系列；G68-2）
ISBN 978-626-7225-79-0（平裝）
1. CST：英語 2. CST：讀本
805.1892　　　　　　　　　114000025

填讀者問卷
送熊贈點

常春藤全民英檢系列【G68-2】
準！GEPT全民英檢中級複試10回高分模擬試題＋翻譯解答（寫作＆口說）－翻譯解答本

總 編 審	賴世雄
終 審	梁民康
執行編輯	許嘉華
編輯小組	常春藤中外編輯群
設計組長	王玥琦
封面設計	林桂旭・王穎緁
排版設計	林桂旭・王穎緁
錄 音	劉書吟
播音老師	Karen Chen・Jacob Roth
法律顧問	北辰著作權事務所蕭雄淋律師
出 版 者	常春藤數位出版股份有限公司
地 址	臺北市忠孝西路一段33號5樓
電 話	(02) 2331-7600
傳 真	(02) 2381-0918
網 址	www.ivy.com.tw
電子信箱	service@ivy.com.tw
郵政劃撥	50463568
戶 名	常春藤數位出版股份有限公司
定 價	230元（2書＋音檔）

©常春藤數位出版股份有限公司 (2025) All rights reserved.　　Y000042-3577
本書之封面、內文、編排等之著作財產權歸常春藤數位出版股份有限公司所有。未經本公司書面同意，請勿翻印、轉載或為一切著作權法上利用行為，否則依法追究。

如有缺頁、裝訂錯誤或破損，請寄回本公司更換。　　【版權所有　翻印必究】